Ms. J Presents Snap Shot.

2021 Edition.

Thank you to the LOVESTORY-L email group for helping me make this better.

Thank you to Brandon Morgan for his art.

Thank you Pastors Derrick Mercer and Derrick Cole for speaking words into my life.

Thank you God for life itself.

Trigger warning: Dear readers, I touch on subjects such as sexual assault, abuse, the foster system, suicide in this work. Please be gentle with yourself if you decide to read this work.

Two broken people cannot make a whole thing.

Chapter One: August 12, 2007

Lucas Keane wanted me dead, don't you get it?

Rosaline Welsh wanted to shout this from the mountain top. The shout remained locked in her body. Her chest ached with each breath. She felt hot to the touch, charred like her last attempt at a romantic dinner for her ex-boyfriend, Lucas. Lucas mocked her domestic skills, now she could mock his. He couldn't roast her alive like he wanted to.

Someone slipped a plastic mask on her face to muzzle her with oxygen.

Someone else looked down at her, talking: "Ma'am, my name is Mike. I'm a first responder. Your apartment was on fire. Can you understand me?"

She only thought of the stars racing into a single point, as if on a racetrack, as she gazed out the windows of what she figured out was an ambulance.

Mike's mouth moved again, "Ma'am, can you tell me if you're hurt?" She must have tried moving because firm hands held her in place. Medical jargon was tossed over her head. She figured she should've been in another country because she comprehended very little around her:

"We'll need a hundred ccs of...plus albumin..."

"The burns cover at least fifteen percent but it may be more. We're estimating between second and third to her torso and face..."

"Smoke inhalation..."

Some spoke of starting an IV. She flinched. Her body fought back.

A third person started dealing out orders: “Calm her down, guys! She’s going into shock!”

Rosaline squeezed her eyes shut when the needle met her vein then allowed the voices to lull her. Right then, it didn't matter if it was sleep or death.

*

The steady beep of monitors told Rosaline she didn’t die.

For what felt like hours, she stared up at the ceiling. People had been constantly in and out of the room she was in. In and out delirium, she heard people talk about the events surrounding her fire and her medical condition.

She heard a knock at the door and tried to speak. Nothing came out except a heavy gasp.

Two doctors entered the room and introduced themselves. Rosaline didn’t bother pronouncing their names. Breathing was a bigger chore. The doctors crafted their words into simple language for her: She would live, but fifteen percent of her upper body— arm, face, hair, side—had sustained burns.

Lucas pushed the shelf on me. He was high.

Rosaline drifted back out of consciousness before she could tell them who gave her those burns.

*

The first day she could make a sound, Rosaline screamed. “Bagel! Bagel! Get out!”

Footsteps followed like a herd. An older white nurse ran into the room. “Oh my—”

All Rosaline focused on was her bandages and continued screaming. Memories of thick smoke and being trapped under her bookshelf suffocated her anew. "We gotta get out! Bagel!"

The nurse moved to help Rosaline lie back down gently. "Honey, you're awake. I think you dreaming' about your fire—"

Daddy may have died in a hospital, but I won't. Rosaline tore at the tubes in her arms before two hefty male nurses came into the room and forced her to comply.

She saw the female nurse stick a needle into a port in one of her tubes then shake a finger at her. "You keep doing that, and they'll send you to the mental health ward."

Sleepiness slammed into Rosaline's chest and she blacked out.

*

Sometime later, Rosaline opened her eyes and found the same nurse from earlier in her room. Heavyset and blonde, the nurse reminded Rosaline of a cartoon hen strutting around a farm.

She licked her dry lips, and a whisper crawled out her throat. "Miss…Miss."

The nurse rushed to her bedside, "Honey, you want something?" The nurse was so Southern, Rhett Butler should have ran into the room also.

"I want…I want out…" She sucked in another breath from the oxygen mask. "Please…"

The nurse puckered her lips. "Honey, we can't just cut you loose. You were in a bad fire. We gotta fix you up, okay?"

She cursed. It was easier to obey her body's cry to heal properly instead of fighting to be free. Rosaline tried a different question. "How long—how long have I been out?"

"Two weeks, honey. They've been keepin' you sedated. You've been in and out of it for days. Tomorrow is your second surgery."

Rosaline blinked. Two weeks? Had it been that long since she was at home, prepping her portfolio for submission? Bitterness swept her. She didn't have a home now thanks to Lucas.

"What is your name? I wanna call you something other than Jane Doe."

Rosaline averted her gaze. Her middle name slipped out instead of her first. "Dana."

Her nurse smiled. "Well, Dana, I'm Mrs. Knowles and you have blood I need to get."

*

Another week passed and more of Rosaline's strength returned.

Mrs. Knowles was here again, helping her eat a bland breakfast when someone knocked at her door. After Mrs. Knowles gave the visitor permission to enter, Rosaline choked on her orange juice. The police? Lucas came to mind. Would he come to Tampa General?

He set the fire, but would he finish her off—?

She calmed her racing pulse. If no one came to visit her as of yet, no one knew she was here. Hell, no one *needed* to know where she was. Rosaline didn't have many people in her world, her two friends Lovely and Tanda were constants. Both of them hated Lucas, especially after their break-up. Besides, the police would keep coming back until she talked to them. Getting out of the hospital was high on her list.

According to the two detectives, the fire wiped out everything of hers, including any of her known identifiers.

Not that I had the good sense to keep renter's insurance, Rosaline shook her head. *Stupid fixed income.* She lay back on her pillow to absorb the rest of their words then began to answer their questions in short sentences. The strain of talking took its toll on her broken body.

She cleared her throat mid-conversation. "Did Bagel get out?"

"Bagel?" One detective repeated her dog's name. "Who is Bagel?"

"My dog. He's a beagle. One good eye. One bad. Bagels are his favorite things to eat—"

"Ma'am, your dog is probably dead. Nothing survived the fire."

Tears stung her eyes. Her disfigured appearance, being injured, the hospital stay—now this new information helped topple her emotional house of cards.

*

This particular day marked her stay in the hospital being a month-and-a-half according to Mrs. Knowles. Her daily routine consisted of dodging personal questions about her life from the nurses and listening to the doctors update her prognosis.

"They're thinking about cutting you loose after you finish therapy." Mrs. Knowles clucked happily.

Rosaline couldn't share in that joy. For the last few days, she dreaded going back to nothing. No apartment, no clothes, no Bagel, not even her portfolio.

Once again, she was the girl that belonged to nobody and had nothing.

*

Rosaline walked down to a lobby when she had the strength and found a phone. After three rings, a pleasant voice picked up.

“Lovely’s on Sunset.” The voice sounded pleasant to potential customers. She imagined the five-foot-eight tall slender woman doing a model-like pose as she held a phone gracefully to her ear. Genes cheated Rosaline in the height department as she stood at her tallest at five-foot-five.

“Hey girl,” Rosaline sounded weak and tired.

“Rosaline!” Lovely Harrington screamed into the receiver. “I tried calling you. I’ve been to your apartment and saw it was burned down and – and I’ve been to every hospital in three towns. No one would tell me anything because I wasn’t family!”

“I’m okay.”

“Where are you? I’m worried about you and…”

“He set the fire,” Rosaline admitted.

“Fire!” Lovely talked so fast, Rosaline barely could get a word in.

Rosaline finally interrupted. “Look, they’re going to release me. I’ll tell you everything, if you pick me up, okay?”

“You better tell me!” Lovely threatened then hung the phone up.

*

A silver Jaguar pulled up to the hospital's pick-up place on the day of her discharge. Rosaline allowed Mrs. Knowles to push her in the wheelchair toward Lovely's car. Lovely and the nurse joined efforts to get Rosaline safely in the front seat with her discharge orders and a single bag of donated clothing.

When they reached Lovely's condo, the two women sat on the couch and talked for the rest of the afternoon. Rosaline consumed half her weight in vegetarian pizza as they talked. Her best friend clutched her mouth as she went through the story, all of the pieces fitting in her mind. "I came home and saw the door open then felt something hit me in the back of my head. Now, I know it had to have been my bookshelf, because I came to and it was on top of me. Lucas must have broken in and pushed the shelf on me. I changed my locks three months ago."

"But, why now? You changed your work hours and everything—"

"I don't know." Even as the lie came out, Rosaline flinched. "Does it matter really why he did it?" She wondered if she was trying to convince herself of the lie more than Lovely. She had a good suspension about why he did it—something she couldn't communicate to her friend.

"You're going to the police in the morning."

Her shoulders sagged. "I've already talked to the police in the hospital. I told them I think it was Lucas. What more do you want me to say?"

"That the bastard needs to be neutered."

She shook her head. Lucas had been to Lovely's place once for a party and had a pretty good memory about how to get back to it. "I can't stay here."

Lovely huffed. "Says who? Terrence? This is my place and you're always welcome here."

“I’m not talking about your man, Lovely.” Rosaline frowned. “I’m talking about the fact that I can’t stay here in Tampa. I gotta leave for a little while.”

Lovely looked down, sucking her thumb by force of bad habit, “Well, at least stay tonight.”

“Of course I’ll stay tonight. I’m too tired to go anywhere. Plus, I miss your lack of cooking. Pizza was great. Terrence is in for a treat with your domestic skills.”

“Shut up.” Lovely smiled at her, looking as if she was forcing herself to talk about anything with Rosaline, other than the burnt pink elephant in the room. Her friend disappeared from the living room for a full minute in the middle of their conversation then returned with a small clutch in Dolce and Gabbana fashion covered with silver metallic hearts and Xs.

Rosaline sat up from her sunken position on the couch, “I left that?”

“Yes,” Lovely huffed, handing it to her.

A quick search of the purse revealed her make-up bag, some cash, sunglasses and a pack of breath mints. Yet, she only focused on two things: An expensive digital camera and a copy of her real birth certificate.

Rosaline squealed in delight, “I thought I lost this!”

“Safe keeping, remember?”

Rosaline hugged her friend. There was something left in this world she could hold on to.

*

Later that night, Rosaline stood in front of Lovely's bathroom mirror. She felt the bald patch where hair had once been then felt her right arm where healthy skin should have been instead of the unsightly white pearly patches mixed with molten pink. The skin grafts only covered so much. The reality of what the fire had done hit her, and ultimately, what Lucas Keane had done caved in on her emotions. She covered her face as heavy sobs escaped.

Minutes later, she heard a knock at the bathroom door. Rosaline wiped her face in haste. "Come in."

"I'm back. Traffic on a Friday is hell." Lovely came in holding two bags. "You'll look cute in the dress and heels I picked out from the shop."

Rosaline glanced at Lovely's lengthy honey-brown hair as if to briefly mourn her loss of hair from the fire.

"Are you ready for me to cut your hair? I don't have to do it—"

"No, do it." Rosaline ordered. "We already talked about this."

Lovely reached inside one of the bags and pulled out a box of hair dye. "Why did you pick fire engine red for your color?"

"So I won't forget what he did."

"How could you?" Lovely reached inside of a drawer and produced a pair of scissors. "Sit down on the toilet and I'll get started…"

Two hours later, red hair dye washed down the drain as Rosaline's locks took on the scent of chemicals. Lovely ended up cutting back what remained of her hair into a short cut that touched her ears. Her eyes flew open at how different a simple cut and color transformed her perspective on life's matters. She gently fingered the corners of the new haircut. Red *was* a good color.

"I think ice cream and a movie would be a good way to celebrate my cosmetology skills." Lovely joked.

Rosaline knew Lovely was trying to take her mind off things. "Good idea. You pick the favor, I'll pick the movie."

*

The next morning, Lovely drove Rosaline over the Howard Franklin Bridge to Saint Petersburg to drop her off in front of the police station.

Lovely's face held apprehension. "Are you sure you don't want me to come with you?"

"Yes. Go home back to Terrence. I'm sure he wants you all back to himself."

Lovely continued to look torn but pulled off to leave Rosaline behind. When she was sure the Jag was out of sight, Rosaline walked past the police station and headed toward the first bus terminal that would take her to the Southside of town. Keeping her friend in the dark wasn't fun, but necessary. She found a few loose dollars for the bus next to the card the police gave her.

Rosaline deposited the card in the trash.

If she learned one thing, Lucas had friends there too.

Her camera was proof.

*

Rosaline had to move fast. Lucas always kept a spare house key in an ugly azalea plant on the front porch of his mother's house just in case he had to… well, Rosaline stopped trying to figure him out months ago. She refocused her efforts on her current mission. Once inside, she sighed in relief. No one was home but the roaches. A quick search of the bedroom he crashed in revealed his car keys.

Rosaline quietly closed the front door, happy that his car was still parked outside. In Lucas's mind, the royal purple-colored Bonneville was too precious to be kept in just anyone's yard with its thousand dollar stereo studio and shiny rims. To think he totaled her Dodge Neon one night because he just wanted to go out to 'clear his head.' *Typical* flashed across her mind as she noticed the spotless, gleaming paint on the car. The bastard spent more money on washing that car than he did on her in the two years they were off and on.

She pulled herself into the present. The college kid who promised to make her a fake ID had a lecture in a few hours.

Rosaline unlocked the door and slid into the driver's seat, throwing her purse into the passenger seat. She hoped Mrs. Keane would give her enough time to get out of town before reporting the car stolen – if the car was even legit to begin with. Now, she remembered why Lovely had her purse in the first place—the white powder she had found in her apartment.

Rosaline turned the ignition over.

Mrs. Keane really was a nice lady who worked hard as a high-school janitor.

She did not deserve a son like Lucas.

***

Chapter Two: September 23, 2007.

"You're leaving." Detective Leland Brown's shoulders stumped.

"Doesn't take that much detective work to get that one," said Detective Hollister Liano.

"And you don't want to stick around? I mean, the outcome could change, man."

"I'm done, Leland. There is no other outcome."

Leland sighed. "End of an era."

"End of my world," Hollister stood among the moving boxes like a widow standing among grave markers. His life was packed away neatly, his condo stripped of any evidence that he ever lived a life in South Tampa.

"Got a new place yet?" Leland wanted to change the subject.

"Yeah, I'm renting a house in Jacksonville."

"Yeah, that's good, real good."

"Don't feel bad for me, all right?"

"Hollister, things – things shouldn't even gone like this."

"They did. I've taken a leave of absence. I'll have a hearing."

"You didn't snap –" Leland began.

Hollister cut him off. “It’s cool. Really. I have something waiting for me. Maybe I’ll come back after a year. My place just isn’t here right now.”

“Be angry, Hollister.”

“Isn’t that the reason why I’m packing?”

*

The trip down I-4 to I-95 North felt very slow the following day. He drove the rental truck loaded with his stuff with a novice’s skill as he towed his white 2000 Toyota Camry. His hands understood quick maneuvering in smaller vehicles like Chevys and Impalas, not a metal monster of a Ford moving truck. Hollister turned over thoughts in his mind as he drove.

Was it better to leave or be fired?

He became a former detective in just a few keystrokes. His letter had some sorry long-winded statement along the lines of *I’m leaving the department to save it face*. Better for the department to sacrifice him in the public eye while cleaning up their own messes quietly. The investigation would take time. Leaving the city all together hurt but it was necessary. He took a leave of absence while internal affairs investigated matters. His badge was on Jeanne’s desk, his desk cleaned out, and his locker empty.

Hollister hit the steering wheel out of anger.

Exit signs for Jacksonville forced him to change lanes, change thoughts. The evening turned to night. He wanted to get the boxes off the truck and the truck back to the moving place tomorrow.

*

The lights on the seven bridges made him smile to himself. Coming into what looked like the downtown area, Hollister had to hit a gas station somewhere. He needed caffeine and sugar to swim in his blood before he went to the new place. He wished his tender eyes could stand bright lights a little more because he would've gladly made this drive during the daylight hours. His prescription Oakley Gasket sunglasses helped. A mental picture of Leland singing "I Wear My Sunglasses at Night" made Hollister grin, then he refocused his efforts to find that gas station.

He ended up on I-10 West only to realize he needed to be heading north. The right should have been a left. Directions were never an issue, but he was distracted by his troubling thoughts. Somewhere near Cassat Avenue, he took an exit to find a brightly lit gas station still open at this hour. The clock flashed midnight at him. At the counter inside the gas station, he confirmed his misdirection and got a correction from the attendant. The attendant talked easily with him for a moment, then allowed Hollister to take his candy bar and straight black coffee to the moving truck.

Hollister noticed something as he glanced in the rearview mirror of the rental truck: A guy in a Gators ball cap grabbed a young boy of ten by the collar of his Superman tee shirt. The Gators wearer shook his fist at the kid. The kid went limp as if refusing to fight back.

The man yelled at the young boy, "I told you to stop kicking my seat or I'll knock your ugly mug off! Quit being stupid like your mama! I hate that!"

The man screamed more. The boy winced as if ready for a hit that was sure to come.

Something inside of Hollister moved through time and space, leading Hollister to push the kid back. Hollister grabbed the man by his own collar. The man in the ball cap looked at Hollister in rage and disbelief, his blue eyes turning to cold ice.

“Hey man, I’ll –” The man started but Hollister cut him off by pulling the collar tighter around the guy.

“Don’t ever jack him up like a grown man.” Hollister growled.

The man in the cap snickered, “What are you gonna do? Karate?”

Hollister’s fist connected with the guy’s nose. Adrenaline pumped through his veins.

The man stumbled around in another breath.

“Hiya,” He spat as his sunglasses slipped off his face.

The man hurried the boy toward a vehicle on pump number three instead of throwing a punch back. “Get in the car!” The man ordered. Both of them disappeared in a cloud of white smoke and skidding tires from a rusted out two-seater. The only thing Hollister remembered in that moment, colored in rage, was the pair of luminous eyes of gratitude from the boy.

Something had crushed within Hollister.

He had wanted to snatch the kid away and save the boy from the same fate.

The attendant ran outside. “You need to get out of here before I call the police.”

He fixed his sunglasses to block out the harsh overhead light. “I am the—” *The police? No, you’re not.* “Hey man, I’m sorry.” Hollister had his hands raised to show he had no weapons then hustled toward the rental truck. He used one of the napkins he grabbed for his coffee to wipe the blood off his hands quickly before leaving.

*

The familiar numbers 11220 from the lease agreement came into view around two am. Hollister yawned. His mind was tired. The coffee and candy bar gave him enough energy to get him home. He let himself into the empty house after grabbing his duffel bag. Hollister drifted off to sleep on the carpet in his new bedroom covered by a blanket. The corners of his mind flirted with a memory about his childhood when he was a boy named Hien.

*

Spring butterflies flew dainty over a boy's head in the garden surrounding a majestic house the boy and his mother walked by.

"Mama, look!"

"Hien, you can see them," The woman laughed.

"They're butterflies!" The boy exclaimed.

"They're beautiful, aren't they?" The woman told her son, "All of their colors and designs, God made them."

"Let's fly away, Mama," Hien told his mother, in an excited tone. "We can become butterflies!"

"We can't fly away, Hien." The woman frowned. "We don't have wings."

"I'll save you, Mama, because I'll fly away with you!"

"Hien," The woman sounded worn by her son's imagination.

*

Hien could fly away, but the man Hien had become had to stay grounded. And eat.

Hollister's stomach cried for adequate nourishment after that fuzzy dream. He threw the blanket back and pulled himself up into a sitting position, recalling a store on his drive last night that was near his street. He started digging in his duffel bag then pulled out some clothing after a long moment. He declined to wear the suit and tie today, normal wear for his detective activities, pulling out a pair of name brand jeans with a short sleeve shirt to match the jean's logo. What was that label again? Coogi or some other brand name Leland dared him to purchase one day from a Tampa urban clothing store. He smirked at the memory of his five-foot-ten African-American friend as if they were still standing in that same store. Hollister wasn't imposing in his mind at five-foot-seven despite the regular exercise regimen of strength training and aikido.

He rustled his unruly dark hair into something he could look at in the bathroom mirror before throwing icy water on his face. A pair of sneakers completed the package as he popped a mint into his mouth. With a slap of deodorant, he put on his squared-framed sunglasses to begin a normal person's day.

*

Two days later, Hollister went to see David Caffee.

The two men shook hands when they met outside.

"I'm telling you, Hollister, security work here is the ultimate cake job. I wasn't cut out to be a cop." David threw his arms out. "Thank God I left Tampa, this is heaven."

Hollister grimaced, studying David's round belly and balding hair. *Cake job? More like the bottom feeder gig*. "So give me a lay of the land, boss."

David gave him a brief tour at the credit card company where Hollister would be working on the night-shift in downtown Jacksonville. Hollister had inquired about such a job for fear that any of the other career skills he used to have had long since dulled. They traded easy conversations about football and where to find a farmer's market in town when Hollister took his leave.

Behind the wheel of his car, key indicators were going off suddenly. First his stomach indicated hunger, then his sweet tooth indicated a need for decadence, only to be followed by the gas needle kissing "E." In northwest Jacksonville, he found a gas station where he could stop.

Hot dogs and candy bars weren't fine dining, but something had to fill the hole in his stomach. He pulled at his tie, ready to change out of his suit due to the heat. It was way past his bedtime he noted after checking his watch.

At the pump, Hollister surveyed the place surrounding him. His car was the only one here during the lunch hour until a purple Bonneville pulled up at a pump opposite his white Camry. The door opened and a pair of black heels matching a designer dress emerged from the car. The mocha-skinned owner of the car had bright red hair and nice diamond studs in her ears.

For some reason, Hollister wanted her to step out of a Lexus. It seemed like a better compliment to her style rather than the loud purple "thug" car.

He closed the gas cap once the tank was full, but not his thoughts. She must have felt his weighty stare in her direction because she looked up with her big stylish sunglasses. He smiled. She gave him a quick flash of teeth then clicked her way inside.

*

When the female clerk started screaming, Hollister kicked into cop mode and was inside the store before he realized it.

“She was just grabbing a soda and she – she went out like a light.” The female clerk couldn’t stop babbling.

Hollister saw the owner of the Bonneville lay sprawled on the dingy floor like a murder victim, lying on her side. He leaned down to check her pulse. He frowned. It wasn’t that strong. Her eyes rolled up toward the ceiling.

“Get an ambulance,” Hollister ordered.

The clerk accepted his authority on the matter and grabbed a phone. A small crowd of customers appeared as if from thin air. Whispers began.

“Everybody stand back! She needs air. Somebody get me some ice and a towel.”

The crowd moved. The clerk hurried back with a makeshift cold compress. He pressed the bag of ice to the fainter’s forehead, covering her legs with a towel after elevating them on a box of past due snack cakes.

Hollister stayed at her side until he saw the familiar flashing blue and red lights fifteen minutes later. The EMTs restored the sense to order as they carefully placed her on a stretcher. He backed up as well, hoping to pass her on to more capable hands.

Someone in the crowd spoke to him. “You decide to play the hero often, buddy?”

“I was a first responder in another lifetime. I just did what was necessary.” Hollister didn’t want to take any glory out of this. He felt far from worthy of any type of praise. A female uniform came on the scene and asked for a statement. Hollister gave the uniform the facts as the EMTs carried the classy fainter out. She could be heard groaning on the way out. The doors shut on the ambulance and it took off.

A semblance of normalcy came back to the gas station.

Hollister decided to leave before anyone else in the now buzzing crowd tried to make him something more than a concerned citizen. Something stuck out in his mind. He saw a ladies' purse lying under a shelf, close to the counter. It must be hers he thought. Hollister snatched the bag up and placed it under his arm.

Was it possible to be both a hero and a thief?

He hurried out the door to his car still happily parked at the pump and jumped inside. "As much as this bag goes with my eyes, I think I better take it back to her." Turning the key, the former detective decided to follow the ambulance.

*

Once he arrived at the hospital, Hollister recounted his tale to the bored security guard at the ER desk. The guard must have thought there was nothing unusual about a man holding the bag of a woman he barely knew, because the guard told him to wait in the lobby. After Hollister disappeared to find a cafeteria and make some phone calls for two hours, the same guard had a nurse lead him down a hallway to a critical care unit. Grateful, Hollister followed the nurse before the guard realized his folly. Hollister certainly wasn't next-of-kin or a blood relation. He was just a guy who found her purse.

He announced himself to a partial closed curtain, standing outside the ER bay. Was she even conscious? "Excuse me, miss?"

"Come in." Her voice sounded tired, but she looked more alert once he stepped behind the curtain. She was lying on the hospital bed with a rough standard issue blanket covering her up to her chest, legs still elevated. A new compress was to her forehead as the saline bag dripped clear liquid slowly. Hollister closed the curtain for privacy. Absent her sunglasses, he could see burn scars, eschars, from the right side of her face trailing down to her neck in patches. Her rolled-up dress sleeves revealed more of them.

She must have known he was gawking at her, "Can I help you?"

What an ironic question. "You fainted."

"Yes, I figured that one out," she pointed to her bag of IV fluid and cold compress.

"And this got left behind," he handed her the purse.

Her eyes lit up. She made no small show of checking it. The woman hugged the digital camera as if it were a long lost friend, carefully studied a folded piece of paper before pulling out a make-up bag and some mints. When she came to her wallet, she pulled the money out first.

"I still have fifty bucks?" she asked, quickly counting her cash.

"Thought it was more," Hollister had looked in her wallet earlier to find an identifier of some type. He knew the amount of cash and so did she.

"Not a thief, I see," she laughed to herself, placing everything back into the purse.

"Not a liar either, I hope, Miss—" Hollister commented, hands in his pockets.

“Miss Cole. You could've left. I heard that someone helped me. Guess you were that person.”

“Didn’t feel right, leaving you there.”

“You could’ve robbed me, too.”

“Not enough for my bills.”

She laughed in spite of the situation, “Not enough for mine either.”

“What made you faint? Did the doctors say?” Hollister wanted to venture more, but someone new came behind the curtain.

“All right ma’am, you know what’s coming,” a pretty nurse said with three empty blood tubes.

The patient balled her fist in a manner that suggested to Hollister that the nurse wouldn’t have to worry about looks for much longer if she came near the woman with any more ominous needles.

After a short standoff, the woman gave up then resumed talking to him. “Sorry, I just feel really worn out by everything that happened today.” It was a thinly veiled cue for him to go.

“Guess I should let the good doctors do their job. I hope you feel better. Take care.”

He left after that, not sure what else to offer her, closing the curtain behind himself.

“Thanks,” Miss Cole yelled as if in an afterthought.

*

The next morning, his cell phone started singing early. “Liano,” he stifled a yawn.

“I didn’t say thank you,” a recognizable female voice was on the other end.

So she did manage to call him. “Actually, I heard you as I left,” Hollister looked at his cell phone screen to confirm it was another day.

“You accidently ‘lost’ your business card.”

“Guilty as charged. I figured you still needed your car,” Hollister remembered leaving one of his cards with his cell number written on the back in her purse.

“Nice thought,” she finally said after a beat.

“I can pick you up and take you back to that gas station. I remember where it is, relative to the hospital.”

“Is that an offer?” She sounded relieved and cautious at the same time at such liberal kindness.

“Unless you want to give me a more formal invitation,” Hollister offered then came to himself, “Or I can call you a cab and I will give you directions. I understand if you don’t trust me,” His voice trailed off for a moment.

Silence again. Another beat passed.

Then she answered, “I guess I’ll see you then.”

***

Chapter Three: September 25, 2007.

Rosaline, you're too many bulbs short of a Christmas tree.

She covered her eyes with her hand, shaking her head.

What was she doing in this man's car, going somewhere in a strange city?

They rode in silence as he drove his Camry. She didn't know how to even begin idle conversation; much less explain what she was doing in Jacksonville. Stealing glances at the way he was dressed, Rosaline could see he was out of place, too – a foreign dude in Southpole jeans and t-shirt with some clean Nike Air Force Ones. He looked like a brother and talked like a white boy. They pulled up to the gas station.

Rosaline panicked and jumped out. "Where's the car? It's the middle of the freakin' day and no one's here at a gas station!"

The guy who introduced himself again as Mr. Liano in the car began walking as she paced aimlessly in place, throwing her hands up and ranting.

He came back a few minutes later.

"Well?" she growled.

He stood coolly in front of her, sunglasses shielding his face. "The place was robbed last night. The sign on the front door says they'll be closed until further notice."

"What?" she snapped.

He pointed to another set of doors on the other side of the building, “See the boards on that set of doors? The crooks must have driven a car through the front doors to gain access –”

“Forget the stupid robbery! Where’s *my* car?” she continued to insist.

“Well, if the place was robbed –” he began, but Rosaline cut him.

“Someone stole it? Someone stole the car!” she began to rant aloud when a thought stopped her. *Someone stole the same car that I stole from Lucas.*

Mr. Liano whipped out his cell phone and walked back toward the sign on the window. He dialed a number, then talked to someone for several minutes. Once he finished his conversation, he walked over to her. His face was obscured by his sunglasses, making it hard to read his face effectively. “The sign had a number for the store’s owner. He thought I had some info about the robbery but I asked about your car. No one took it.”

A sigh of relief escaped her, “Okay. So where is it?”

“The owner had it impounded,” he calmly answered.

Rosaline‘s jaw dropped.

“Something about the car being here illegally parked for more than twenty-four hours.”

She groaned and covered her face. “Nooo.”

“Miss –” he ventured.

“Dana, just call me Dana.” Rosaline was annoyed with the new revelation that she was now stuck in Jacksonville, annoyed at lying about her name, annoyed at her own stupidity in general. She couldn’t claim a car that wasn’t hers in the first place.

“Dana, is there somewhere I could take you? He gave me the name of the impound place. Maybe you can get it out. Besides, you might faint again. You should get out of this heat and eat something solid. I’m sure you’ll be able to figure something out then.”

She *did* need to think. Her dry throat and empty stomach cried for attention. She needed to stop attracting a whole lot of unwanted attention for the both of them from the small crowd of people coming to read the sign. Rosaline threw her hands up in defeat. “Let’s go.”

Mr. Liano reached for his keys.

*

Rosaline had to give Mr. Liano his props. He wasn’t a cheap man. Instead of a typical burger joint, he found a tiny Italian restaurant. She drank enough water to make her insides swim and polished off the large chicken Caesar salad in minutes.

He lightly tapped his fork to his plate as if in deep thought. “When was the last time you ate?”

“I don’t even remember,” Rosaline threw out, studying his half-eaten baked ziti. She only remembered being in the cheap motel room in Jacksonville for two days before she ended up taking her fall. Maybe she ate some take-out or some potato chips as she planned to find the Times building in town. “Hospital food will make anybody lose weight.”

“Please excuse my curiosity, but I’ve got to ask. How long have you been out of the hospital?”

She decided to toss him this one bone, “A month. I wanted out and went against medical advice. I know I had two weeks of therapy left, but—”

“You left against the doctor's orders simply because you didn’t want to be there?” He shook his head as if in disapproval.

“I hate hospitals. That’s all,” she commented, feeling her knuckles get tight and sweaty in panic.

Mr. Liano pulled her out of her thoughts. “I apologize but you don’t look well.”

“Good observation!” she laughed, “You should be a detective.”

He swallowed his last bite of ziti, stared at his plate then continued. “I think you left the hospital too soon. Your body’s paying for it.”

“I’m not going back.”

“Okay, but what are you going to do? Keep fainting on me?”

Her gaze met his square-framed sunglasses. Now they both seemed to know her truly vulnerable position. He waited for an answer.

She looked away finally. “I don’t know.”

He started tapping the fork against his plate again.

Rosaline covered her face in shame. *Trapped*, she thought. “The car’s not mine.”

A sense of relief suddenly released across the table like the scent from a bottle of sweet perfume opened in the mall. His jaw relaxed. He calmly paid the check, and took a swig of cherry soda as she took a moment to try and locate a steady thought in her own head.

“Anything else you want to tell me, Miss Welsh?”

Her head popped up, “I’m not…” She stopped.

He placed his glass down on the table, finishing her sentence, “…Dana Cole. You insist I call you Dana, but the birth certificate says Rosaline Welsh.”

Rosaline searched her memory… He gave her back her purse at the hospital. She must have placed both the real birth certificate and her fake driver’s license next to each other by accident in the motel room… His card had been inside her purse… He had looked inside her purse.

Caught. The word raced across her head.

She sat back in her chair with defeat resting on her belly.

“You’re not being totally honest. I just want to know why.”

“Why do you care if I lied about my name? So what, you a cop or something?” Angry words spilled out of her mouth.

He folded his hands on the table. “You didn’t read the other side of my card. *I was*.”

She wanted to laugh at her situation, as if this life wasn’t her own. It seemed funny, hearing herself admit to a former cop that she has a fake ID in her wallet right now.

But only one thought remained: *Screwed.*

*

As the afternoon moved into evening, he turned on the lights in the darkened room of what he described as his current home. Rosaline slowly entered the living room, stopping in the center. He must have locked the door behind them from what her ears picked up.

If a guy shuts a door behind you when you go into a room with him… Lovely gave her that warning one night in Ybor on how to be tipped off if a guy wanted to sleep with you. Rosaline wondered how much she'd had to drink that night and whether she really listened to that piece of advice. Lucas was in Ybor a few times…She noted how empty the room felt. Boxes all around, a couch, a loveseat. No personal effects in his home.

Now her mind blurred: He was a cop. A crazy ex-cop who was going to kill her and leave her for dead in an empty house. She would exist as a Jane Doe in a file in a hospital far away and never get a second chance to see Lovely again…

"Excuse me, Miss Welsh?"

Mr. Liano – if that was his real name – jolted her from her fatalistic thinking. He stood in the room. She felt the intense stare focused upon her.

Rosaline looked at him as calmly as possible, "You're going to kill me and stuff me in your backyard."

He started laughing loudly after a long pause.

She backed up to the nearest wall, trying to edge her way to the front door to get away. Would she remember how to unlock a door in fright?

Mr. Liano didn't make a move. He placed his hands in pockets, watching her from behind those sunglasses. His sunglasses still concealed his facial expressions. Did he have a face? Her mind mocked her, *did evil need a face?*

He cleared his throat once more. "Miss Welsh, if I was a killer, then you would have been in a ditch on Highway 301. Burying you in my new backyard would be tacky. I wouldn't shoot you. I would use something bloodless and silent."

Rosaline blanched, he was serious!

Of course, he would know something about how to get rid of people. He was a cop and dealt with sick people like that. The thought made her feel faint again.

"You're a cop," she blurted out. She made it to the door, her hand gripping the deadbolt.

"*Was*. *Was* a cop," he corrected, "Promoted to detective after five years. Major crimes unit."

She continued talking hoping to distract him long enough to get away.

"Define *major*." She felt her fingers manipulating the cool metal lock, turning it until it opened.

He still didn't move. "Narcotics. Sex crimes. Domestic violence…"

The room turned black again. A set of strong arms looped around her.

"We've gotta stop talking like this." His words floated above her head like a lost kite going up.

*

The kite of his words came down to earth.

Rosaline stirred. Coming to, she figured out she was on his couch in his living room. She never made it out the door.

Time slipped from her. Had it been a few hours?

A hand floated above her face. She looked up to see Mr. Liano leaning over her as he kneeled by his couch.

She tried to pull away, but her limbs refused to obey as he touched her forehead.

"Am I burning up?" Her voice cracked.

Maybe she should obey, Rosaline reasoned internally. Besides, if he wanted to kill her, she wouldn't have been awake.

"Not now you aren't," he commented, his face coming into view. "You're sweating too much."

"Mrs. Liano will kill you for taking care of strange helpless women."

"I'll be happy to meet her. I'm not married."

"Sorry, I assumed–"

"Hollister. Please, Hollister," he insisted, helping her sit up on the couch. "I'm not a detective. Make sure you drink a lot of fluids today. I'll leave you something to drink near the couch."

She heard the way he brushed past her inquiry fast. "A long story?"

The smile on his face seemed bitter, out of a memory she was not permitted to understand, "Maybe just as interesting as your story."

He still looked out of place in his hip-hop clothing. She wanted him to look like a math teacher again in his black suit and tie. The sunglasses made him look like a television cop. What did his face really look like? Why was he still wearing them and not a lick of sunshine was coming into the house?

"I'll get you some Gatorade. Electrolytes and all." Mr. Liano gave orders. Not too many wasted words. No idle talk seemed permitted.

"Mmm." Rosaline settled into the couch more.

"You need to go back –" he began, standing to his feet.

"I'm not going back and don't say it again." Hostility instantly colored her tone.

"What did they do to you to make you hate them so much? Drop you? Hematoma?" he shouted from another part of the house she guessed was the kitchen.

"I don't like hospitals," she growled, remembering her own father.

He came back into the room with a bottle in his hand. "Should I worry about a jealous boyfriend? You seem to be gone from somewhere for too long,"

Rosaline buried her face in a couch cushion. A killer boyfriend had begun her wracked-out journey with burned footsteps. A gentle hand shook her shoulder once more.

"Why are you helping me? What about the ditch on 301?"

He didn't flinch at the question like she wanted. No offense in his manner, no embarrassment. "If nothing else, it's the decent thing to do."

“Having me, a thief with a fake ID lying on your couch,” she groaned out of fatigue.

“I don’t think your heart was into your crime. Besides, as sick as you are, the ER is enough punishment.”

“I’m not going –” she began but he cut her off.

“I know, I know,” he said in a worn tone, “And I’m tired of hearing it.”

Rosaline started talking but realized her words were slurring together like she had spent too long of a weekend in Ybor City, “…Idon’tplanonbeingherelongdetective.”

***

Chapter Four: September 27, 2007.

Hollister managed to arrange the blank slate of a living room into a living space that was functional for him. *So many boxes. So little time.* He sighed and closed the box cutter, then slipped it into his back pocket. *Why can't the unpacking and decorating just animate itself and be done with?*

His "guest" groaned in her sleep.

She slept all afternoon.

No matter how many times Hollister dropped a tool or dragged a box from room to room, she slept. Even when he loomed over her with a blanket, she would not wake up. Sometimes, she would whisper into the cushions or cocoon herself into the blanket more. He checked her breathing from time to time, battling the fear that he would find her dead on the couch from fever.

Night fell. She stirred long enough to drain whatever bottle Hollister placed next to the couch then resumed sleeping. His stomach soon reminded him that his sandwich only lasted so long. The decision to throw some shrimp and noodles together hit him when he passed by the kitchen again. He had a plate in his hand when a scream forced him to drop his dish. He ran into the living room to find Rosaline clutching the blanket up to her neck.

Hollister's eyes combed the house for danger. His grip tightened on the box cutter. The blade was still exposed.

"What happened to my clothes?" she demanded, shaking.

His mind wandered back to last night as he exhaled. He closed his box cutter, allowing adrenaline to flow back into the part of his brain reserved for "cop mode." “Trash can. Thought it might be restricting your breathing. That’s why you’re wearing the robe."

Her eyes widened as she clutched the blanket around herself tighter in defense of her remaining modesty. "*You touched me*." The daggers in her eyes told him that her stare was sharper than his little old box cutter. She added venom to her next words: "Son of—."

"You're welcome." Torn between not caring if she was upset and outraged at her accusation, he put his weapon away. His hands needed control now—just like they did hours before when he fumbled with the silky yet tight black dress. Every cut he had made with the scissors made him cringe. The war between a strong will and base flesh hit a fever pitch once he had to pull the shredded fabric away from her body.

She looked under her robe to inspect herself.

"Trust me, it's all hooked and fastened in the right places." Hollister tossed over his shoulder as he fled the room. The only mess he could clean up at the moment was the one in the kitchen.

*

The color of her bra flashed across his mind.

You dog.

His face grew hot at such a bold thought running deep within him. Hollister jumped in the icy water and scrubbed quickly, drowning his head under the manufactured waterfall. He started scrubbing as if he had to scrub the very thought off his skin.

I'm using my Miranda rights, my right to remain silent. Hollister switched the COLD knob to an off position. He wanted to respect Rosaline by thinking with the correct head. Especially when he could tell that someone else hadn't.

Hollister grabbed a clean towel.

As a former EMT translated into law enforcement, seeing women stripped down to their bare essentials was a normal byproduct of the job. Women in those circumstances were far distant cries from the word "sexy." The aftermath of rapes, brutal murders, and track lines on druggies did not turn him on. He spent ten years of his life dealing with the underbelly of human nature, trying to understand why people hurt one another and hurt themselves.

Burn eschars were obvious on Rosaline. She told him that she was in a fire.

But the real prize would be the answer to the most pressing question he had now: Would she tell him who had been beating her?

He thought about the fake ID, her avoidance of his questions. She had to be running away from someone she was afraid of. Was the guy an old pimp that kept her hooked on drugs? An abusive ex-lover? Was she young enough to be a runaway even though she looked like she was still in her twenties?

Would she admit to being abused?

Could she trust me?

Cop mode would not just turn off. He had been Detective Liano back in Tampa for five years. Currently, he was just Mr. Liano and getting too nosy for his own good.

What do you care? She has her secrets and you have yours.

Stop trying to atone for your own sin.

The little boy at the gas station came back to memory. Now the mission solidified in his brain before he could stop it. If he could just stop whatever she was running from then he would feel whole once more. If he could help her in this last ditch effort to protect and serve, then he could recapture the feeling he left with his badge on Jeanne's desk. That feeling of right and dignity and strength he craved would return. He stood in front of the large vanity mirror hanging above the sink with the towel thrown around his waist.

Maybe this time his rescue would not be too late.

*

During the night, he heard noises coming from the house. Once out of bed, Hollister stalked down the hallway to find Rosaline leaning against the wall heavily. Each breath she let go sounded heavier than the first.

"You okay?" He tried to sound unmoved even though his concern started rising.

"I just need a little help just to get in the bathroom. Please."

He crossed the hall and laced his arm through hers. They made their short trek to the bathroom door. He hit the light. She made her way to the toilet, standing near it.

"Got it after this, right?" Hollister stood in the doorway and steadied himself for a verbal assault.

"I need something to wear. My suitcase was in the car too. I feel nasty. Sweating and sticking to your couch."

He tried to lighten the mood. "You weren't really stinking. Maybe a little funk."

Rosaline pulled the robe closer around her, holding a wry smile on her lips, "An old t-shirt and shorts will do."

"I can handle that."

"Unless one of your girlfriends left something particularly nice around here."

"Cheeky." He left the room to fulfill her request.

*

Hollister left the clothing by the bathroom and knocked on the door as a signal that it was waiting on her. He took a seat on his couch, leaning his head back to rest his eyes. The sound of the door opening shook him from his cat nap. He helped Rosaline get back to the living room to sit down. The borrowed gym outfit swallowed her. Without her heels on, she was actually shorter than him.

"Feel better?" he asked, suppressing a yawn.

“Yeah, thanks.” she nodded.

He stood up to leave, but she called his name again. He looked back.

"I was wrong to be mean." Rosaline looked down at the wooden floors. “Especially to think that you… or tried to…”

"Water under the bridge."

"Your couch is comfortable and all, but is there somewhere else I can sleep right now?" She seemed embarrassed to even be asking, "Look, Detective Liano or Mr. Liano…"

"Please, Hollister, like I said before."

"Hollister," she tried the name on her tongue, repeating it again as if it didn't sound right. "Why do you keep correcting me if I call you that?"

"Being called Mister or being called Detective?"

"Either one, try me." She said with her arms folded.

His skin pricked uncomfortably at her words. "Later today, I will grab you some appropriate clothing so you do not have to leave the house. Then we can find out what to do next." Hollister pushed his anxiety out his mind and helped her to her feet. "The room with all the boxes in it should be my office. There's a third bedroom with a futon in it for a guest. And you're somehow the first guest. I'll help you get to it."

***

Chapter Five: October 15, 2007.

The blistering summer heat closed out into a kinder fall in Jacksonville. Rosaline walked back into Mr. Liano's—Hollister's house to find the bathroom mirror. She combed her short bob to look like something other than the nightly mess on the pillow. Her plan was—well, she didn't have many plans. Ever since she ended up fighting her fever, she had been bed-ridden.

Be honest about the bruises. You know he saw them.

Rosaline studied her left arm. An inward cringe followed. Fulfilling Hollister's requests, she was quiet during the day and dutifully locked herself up in his house every night while keeping her wounds clean and her body hydrated.

Her finger absent-mindedly traced one of her bruises. The one on her arm came from—Rosaline stopped herself. She didn't need to relive every hit. It was nobody's business what happened to her.

*

It took much begging and pleading to get the man she began calling "Supercop" to get her out of her prison. Later that afternoon, the two of them hit a women's clothing store. Between clothing changes, Rosaline peeked out the dressing room curtain to get a chuckle. The stone-faced expression he wore while he paced outside of the dressing room made her laugh, it was good medicine.

"Why did you have to come to this store?" He sounded like he was talking to a suspect.

She threw a blouse at him. “Because your taste in ladies’ clothing sucks.”

“I’m not your stylist.” His sunglasses gave him a menacing look as he caught it.

She shook the sudden goosebumps off. When he spoke, it did something to her skin. “Last outfit, I promise. Then I’m going to the cash register.”

“I think I liked you better when you were sick. Less back talk.”

Rosaline shut the curtain and changed. She was so proud of the last outfit she created, the decision to wear the entire ensemble out the store was an easy decision.

Fifteen minutes later, a giddy Rosaline hopped into the passenger side of Hollister’s Camry and admired herself in the rearview mirror.

He gave her a funny look after he slid into the driver’s seat.

She sucked her teeth. “Did the fire disfigure me so badly that I need to be in the circus?”

He looked away. “No, you look—human.”

She must have been confused with the thought that she was still desirable. Her vanity aptly told her she didn’t need the “detective’s” opinion about the new capris and baby tee. A business card lying on the floorboard caught her attention.

Rosaline read the first lines of the card. “Are you sick or something?”

“No.” He snatched the card out of her hand when they were at a stoplight.

“Okay, I’ll stop being nosy.”

“You do that,” he said with some edge.

"Sometimes, detective, I think you get up on the wrong side of the bed."

"I work at night."

"Doesn't excuse your behavior." Then she smiled. "Love the suit by the way."

Rosaline imagined that the look he was giving her now must have been withering. The ugly dark blue monkey suit with an equally horrible tie and black slacks was the standard uniform of the security company he worked for. The matching ugly hat laid on the backseat.

He sneered. "Overtime. And yet I managed to have time to sweep you up, Cinderella."

"Your kindness touches me." She mocked in a saccharine tone.

They continued to pass this verbal hot potato back and forth until they pulled up to his home. Sitting in the driveway, she knew Hollister expected her to get out. She would use her house key and he would drive off. But Rosaline suddenly snatched his car keys out of the ignition while they were stopped.

"Adding grand theft again?" He watched her shake his keys at him.

"You're going to work. Let me drop you off."

"To do what?"

"I want air. It's Friday night. Let me explore Jacksonville."

He reached for his keys. "No thanks."

She pulled them out of his reach. "Come on, I'm getting cabin fever!" Now she sounded like a teenager begging for permission to do something on her own.

Hollister let go of a long breath. “Not funny.”

“Not laughing. You trust me in your own home but not with your ride? I’ve been good with the house keys, Dad.” Rosaline’s grip tightened on the keys for both of them to see.

“Trust is earned.”

She had his trust, Rosaline thought to herself. What she needed to earn was his humanity. He needed to laugh some, let loose.

She had an idea that worked during childhood – wear his resistance down.

Rosaline dashed out of the car and engaged both of them in a kiddy chase around the parked car as she played keep-away with his keys. Rosaline should have figured she was the only one finding humor in this when she miscalculated a step in the wrong direction. He pulled her by the arm, forcing her to back up into his car. During the chase, she figured she must have knocked his shades off by accident—an accident that left her wedged between the car and a muscular former detective. Rosaline wanted to faint then. Without the shades in the fading daylight, she caught a glimpse of his smooth face and ink-colored eyes framed by spiky black locks. His dark eyes simmering with anger she wished she hadn’t stirred up. She turned her head and squeezed her eyes shut. His heavy breathing felt like fire going down her neck. She braced for a hit.

Her voice crawled back into her hollow throat. “I’m-I’m-I’m sorry.”

Hollister let her loose, found his shades and stormed into the house.

***

Chapter Six: October 16, 2007

Hollister found Rosaline in the living room the next day, lying on her belly with an empty bowl and a magazine next to her. When she realized Hollister had come into the room, she tried to get to her feet quickly. A flash of something in her eyes told him she did not want to see him.

"Wait!" Hollister cried. A memory of yesterday flooded him— he only hoped to slow her down, not use the same force he would use with a suspect. Tell her she was being childish for being stuck in his house while he worked long hours. The look of fear she gave him made him sick inside.

"I'll leave you alone," she added in a flat tone.

"Actually, I'm going to grab some ice cream." He tried to wave the white flag by speaking in a kind tone.

"Have fun," Rosaline brushed past him.

He stepped in front of her to block her from leaving. "Come with me." he held his hands up in a surrender gesture.

"Save the kindness for someone who cares," she gave him a cold shoulder, forcing herself by him. She dropped the magazine on the kitchen table and threw the bowl in the sink.

"Rosaline, please," Hollister turned to follow her.

"You really do feel bad, don't you?" Rosaline threw her hands up, confronting him.

He wanted her to cuss him, tear his eyes out. He needed to repent for this latest crime. "I know this isn't the greatest apology, but at least let me help your cabin fever out tonight. *Please*."

She gave him a look that could have left him for dead. Maybe her damning silence would be his penance.

*

They stepped into the ice cream parlor around nine near the strip mall. Rosaline stood with her arms still folded, weight shifted onto one foot. Her annoyance simmered to a slow boil. She wore a pink tee and flared jeans. The heels gave her a sassy quality he wanted to compliment her on but wasn't sure how she would take it. They stood in line awkwardly, ordered separately, but Hollister made sure he picked up the check. She gave him a look that hailed of "I-am-woman-hear-me-roar." But she also allowed him to pay, even though there was some untold amount of cash in her purse somewhere. Maybe that was the roar, getting him to pay for things out of obligation or guilt. *Women,* Hollister mused.

They took a seat in the back corner, far from the crowd. He savored the mint chocolate chip ice cream while watching her delicately tackle some creation of vanilla and gummy worms.

"You're forgiven. The ice cream was a nice gesture," she remarked.

"I'm trying," Hollister shrugged.

"Thanks for looking like Mr. Evans."

"Mr—who?"

"My math teacher in high school," she gave him a tiny smile.

“I’ll take that to mean something positive,” Hollister smiled then studied the button-up shirt and khakis he threw on. It was a preppy day or laundry day, whichever hard truth came first.

Idle conversation passed between them. Her face lit up when she talked about photography. His voice turned sour as he discussed what he did in the private sector as a toy cop. Once they reached the bottom of their bowls and their words, Hollister noticed it was getting late.

“Rosaline –”

“Yes?” She asked in a sugary tone.

“This sounds left field, but no one has the right to hurt you or make you feel bad.”

She kept playing with the spoon in the empty bowl. “Look, Supercop, it’s okay. I should grow up every now and then. It’s your house, your keys. I shouldn’t have taken them.”

Hollister reached across the table and gently began rolling up her shirtsleeve. On the left side.

“What are you doing?” she moved to free her arm.

“Hoping you’ll trust me,” Hollister continued rolling.

He heard her suck in a breath, growing perfectly still. The rolled-up sleeve revealed the subject of his deep curiosity–old bruises that must have come from human hands.

Yet fresh with a pain, he imagined, because Rosaline finally jerked her arm away. “My other arm is burned. I was in a fire.” Her sweet tone turned to dung.

“That’s not what I’m talking about.” He sat back in his chair, speaking with care, “I’m slow sometimes, but I’m not stupid. Ten years as a cop and you learn a little something. Whoever hurt you can't now. There's enough distance between you and that person. Just listen to me, and if you still don't care, I'll help you leave."

Rosaline's mouth hung open as if the door to her life was swinging on the hinges, exposing all those things that she fought to hide. "What does this –"

"You ran from whatever or whoever gave you those bruises and that fire has a lot to do with it. I could find out through my sources but I'd rather you tell me the story."

"What is there to tell?" A wild hostility emitted from her.

"If you start being honest about it like you were about being Dana, then you'll never know how much better you can be. If you think that I'm going to turn you in over the car and the ID, I'm not. But do you really believe he's going to find you somehow?"

Rosaline jumped out of her chair, "You just can't let it go!"

"You haven't." Hollister countered. They were both on their feet. He finally put the question that troubled him personally in the air. Hollister dropped his voice, "Why did you think I was going to hit you?"

Rosaline refused to look into his eyes. "You only hit me when you're mad, Lucas—" Her eyes were glassy as she shook violently.

"This Lucas, he did it then? He left the bruises?" Hollister felt the breaking of the day in her words.

Rosaline bolted out of the store. Hollister grabbed his keys from the table and followed her, calling after her.

Somewhere in a far-off place in the parking lot where few cars sat, Rosaline came to a halt. His pursuit skills felt rusty, but he found her.

She spun around to find herself face to face with Hollister again, her chest heaving. "You reached your embarrassment quota. I want to go. I just want to go!"

Hollister finally caught his breath long enough to speak with some reason. "I'm not here to put you out there for shame or because this is funny or whatever you think I'm trying to do, Rosaline Welsh or Dana Cole or whoever you want to be. The night you slept on my couch, I saw them after I changed your clothes. I couldn't help but notice them… I was a detective for too long not to notice them…" Hollister threw his arms up. "I've been *me* too long not to notice them."

With the fierceness of a cat after a snake, she lunged at Hollister. Rosaline unleashed whatever pent-up resentment she had on him fully in that parking lot. Kicking, punching and stabbing with her nails. Hollister went into defensive mode to block the blows she threw with her fists and words, "Bastard! I hate you!"

Hollister managed to pin her arms between her chest and his, wrapping them both up in a strange embrace. His shades went off somewhere in the struggle as he kept his voice as soft as the lights above them in the parking lot. "*I know you want somebody to know* he hurt you."

Hollister pulled her into his arms as she cried loud and long.

***

Chapter Seven: October 17, 2007.

Rosaline forgot how they got back to the house after midnight.

They had managed to leave the scene without the cops being a part of it. She only remembered screaming and crying and hating every man walking the earth.

She locked herself into his bathroom to wash away the day. She wanted to scrub away the outbursts full of shame, the memory of Lucas Keane, and the reality that Detective Hollister Liano knew the truth. Under the warm water, she kept crying. She felt dirty and used. She used to scrub hard when she showered, hoping to get Lucas' residue off her skin. But now, she couldn't scrub hard enough to get rid of the defeat from her breakdown. She turned the water off and pulled a clean towel around herself. Rosaline covered her face with her hands, hoping to hold what was left together. She felt the redness from crying burning the whites of her eyes out.

A knock on the door followed. "It's been an hour. Are you okay?"

She didn't answer.

"Please open the door," the voice asked her gently.

Rosaline got to her feet and snatched the door open.

Hollister stood there, his shirt stained with a smear of her mocha foundation and his hands buried deep in his pockets. He turned his head to look away. "I'll let you get dressed."

"I've got hundreds of other bruises you missed. Just stand there and I'll pull this off –" She yanked at the cotton until it slid down her side, exposing everything beneath it.

He moved with the quickness of a cat and tied the towel around her like a cocoon. “Stop.”

She squirmed to get free. “What for? I’ve already been humiliated. What’s left to hide?”

He kept her in that same embrace from earlier—tight enough to prevent her hits, but not tight enough to hurt her. “The bruises tell what you’re too scared to say to me.”

“Just leave me alone. I was fine before I met you!”

Big black spots swirled before her eyes before she felt everything go horizontal.

*

The world came back into focus later. She tried to grasp reality and time. Everything still looked dark. Rosaline lifted her head and touched something soft—a pillow. She’d realized she ended up in the guest room, still wrapped in the bath towel and covered by a blanket. Eyes adjusting in the dimness, she made out Hollister’s form as he sat on the floor with his back against the wall.

His voice pulled her back to Earth. “It’s four am.”

She sat up slowly. “I fainted again, didn’t I?”

“You had a little too much excitement. My shirt makes great leverage for fainters to grab so you didn’t hit the floor this time. I laid you down on the futon.” Footsteps filled the room. He sat on the edge of the mattress then touched her forehead. "How’s sitting working for you?"

"I don’t feel like hurling. That might be a plus."

Shafts of moonlight entered the bedroom. The silvery light revealed that he wasn’t wearing his sunglasses. An internal struggle built inside of her to equally punch him and caress his face.

"I'm taking you to a doctor in the morning. I don't care how you feel about this."

She lay back down. "You win. I'll go."

"I apologize for pushing too hard. You weren't ready to talk."

"I was never ready." The admission came from her lips.

His voice wrapped around her like her blanket. "I helped rip the scab off your pain. Maybe now we can work on healing it." He got to his feet.

She grabbed his arm with a demanding tug to keep him from leaving. "How?"

He freed himself. "We'll just have to find out, won't we?"

*

The cell phone would not quit singing. Rosaline rolled over on the futon feeling groggy. Sunlight slapped her in the face. The fruitless wish for Hollister to stay with her in the guest room remained on the edge of her mind. She wondered if he was able to sleep through her nosy ringtone when she couldn't. She finally picked up on the fifth ring. Was it already noon? "Yeah?"

"Rozy?"

"Lovely?" Rosaline perked up a little. "Hey girl, where are you?"

"In South Beach doing a show. I figured I needed to check up on you."

Rosaline tried to sound upbeat. "Thanks. Your show sounds fun."

"Please! The sorry photographer I used to get the models' headshots nearly ruined my chance to get an entry. I needed you! You're cheap!"

"Aww, you just know how to flatter a girl."

"You know I'm talking about your prices."

"I know. I was just making a funny."

A pause followed. "Cut the act, are you crying?"

"Huh?"

"Rozy Raz, are you crying? I hear it in your voice."

"What are you talking about?"

"Who made you cry?" Lovely was not letting up. "It better not be Lucas—"

"No, no! I'm—I'm just tired. I had to see a doctor earlier today. The burns are healing, but I've been a bad girl and haven't taking care of myself. Being sick sucks." Rosaline sat up and watched the covers bunched around her knees. "Hey, I'll let you go. Enjoy the party."

She laid back down on the futon, dreaming about model catwalks and flashbulbs. An hour later, the phone rang again. "The party's getting better, Love?" she asked as soon as she picked up the phone, "What's the gossip?"

"I shoulda put my Beretta to your head and pulled the trigger."

Rosaline's blood froze. This wasn't her friend. "Who gave you my number?"

“Tell your friend Tanda thanks. You buy a girl a few daiquiris in the club and it all goes to her head.”

“Go to hell, Lucas.”

“I’m already here.”

“I’ll be changing this number, too.”

“And you’ll be stupid enough to talk to Tanda again. You still want to take your little pictures and I know you’ll be lookin’ for a photography gig. You can’t get away from me—”

Rosaline threw her phone at the wall and cried.

***

Chapter Eight: October 18, 2007

Hollister checked the clock again after tossing in bed for the fifth time.

Four in the afternoon was too early to get up for work. His mind kept going back to that towel hitting the bathroom floor. He cursed. The lavender body wash he purchased for her drove his imagination crazy. His senses went out of whack when he pulled her closer. He wanted to make her forget whoever gave her those reminders of past pain and dry those tears away.

She hates you and you're the real fool for going there.

Sunlight touched the windows of the house. His internal clock warned him to think about sleep, not a half-naked woman trembling in his arms.

Hollister closed his eyes but couldn't sleep.

*

He wondered what was waiting for him on the other side of the door now. *If* she was awake.

Seconds later, she opened the door and was blessedly dressed in a large shirt and jeans. "It's your house, why knock?"

"I wasn't sure if you were decent."

"You can come in."

"Actually, I was going to make a food run before work. No time to cook breakfast. Are you hungry? Want water or anything? Dr. Hayes said you need to stay hydrated too."

“I’m good. I can find something in your kitchen later.”

“Okay, cya,” he turned to pull the door closed.

“Hollister?”

Hollister opened the door again. “Yeah?”

She stared at the floor. “He called me.”

His eyes narrowed. “What?”

She turned away and walked over to the futon, flopping down on it. “I can’t believe that my friend Tanda gave him my number after I asked her not to. *I should have killed you*. That’s what he told me.”

He stepped into the guest room and took a seat next to her. “Do you want to talk about it?”

Rosaline studied her left arm. The bruised arm. “I don’t know. We fought so much.” Her voice drifted out in a memory.

“Lucas was your ex then?”

“Lucas Keane is a bastard.” The venom in her words set him on edge for a moment.

“Did anybody else know?”

“Just my best friend, Lovely. She saw the bruises, too. I couldn’t tell anyone else. Even the cops got sick of me calling.”

Hollister studied his hands. They looked shiny from sweat. “You reported it. That’s more than some women.”

“I should have never provoked him.”

“What?”

“I always did something to him –”

“Any man weak enough to start abusing a woman should be castrated with a dull kitchen knife.”

“It takes two to tango.”

“And only one to hit.”

“We just – fought. I know I got to him.”

“Making excuses for him won’t stop the pain you suffered. *He beat you*.”

“We were just rough with each other. Rough love, I guess.”

“Did he ever rape you?” The question leaped out of Hollister’s mouth so fast, he looked away as if to say to her he didn’t want to ask that question.

She fumbled over her words. “Things were… one time… he…”

Hollister growled. “I put a lot of guys in jail over rough sex. He had no right to touch you.”

Rosaline jumped, her defense sounded diluted. “I would’ve known if he did something like that.”

“I don’t think you understand that what this prick did to you was wrong.”

“You think I liked being hit?”

“No, I think he twisted your concept of abuse. He left bruises you can’t see. Ones you can’t cover with make-up. Whatever he did to you is going to take a lot of unraveling.”

Rosaline stood. “So you got your way. I was honest about the bruises.”

Hollister rose to his feet as well. The air around him promised some storm of rage he did not desire her to witness. “I’m sorry that he hurt you.” He wanted to break Lucas’s neck for her. “And I wish it wasn’t the truth.”

*

Hollister flushed the toilet. He felt sick, sick, sick. He replayed their conversation over and over and over and over…

Lucas Keane. He had that name on mental file. Lucas Keane filed some nasty bruises on Rosaline’s skin. He left damages filed on her wholeness and her memories.

Hollister wiped his mouth and kept his back to the wall to steady himself. He couldn’t even hold down his lunch during his break time. The years he spent as a detective robbed him of emotions when he encountered women like Rosaline. No more outrage and pity remained in his heart for these crimes. Now he was paying for having the button to these emotions fixed in the OFF position for so long: The suspect’s son. The boy at the gas station. Rosaline.

Hollister gazed at himself under the harsh artificial lights in the bathroom at work.

He had been Lan’s son too long not to notice a woman with scars.

*

Lan Luu sat at the table in her home. All of the joy in the world seemed to just be beaten out of her. Her ebony locks hid the black eye, busted lip and finger marks around her neck.

She was pretty once, but the hideous world behind her front door marred the family.

Hien ran into the house and disrupted his mother's thinking. "Mama?"

"Hien," Lan hastily wiped her tears away. "Why aren't you in school?"

"The missionaries let us out early. The bad men told them to leave. Before they blow them away," Hien relayed this information to his mother.

Attacks. The restlessness of the War that just passed in Lan's homeland. The same war that crushed Han. The dirty blanket of the defeat hung over Hanoi mournfully. This would be the last day Hien would be wearing his uniform to the mission school.

"Go play, Hien. I need to be alone," Lan ordered.

"But it's about to rain. I don't see butterflies or kites or Daddy –"

"Then go to your room! Go somewhere! Just anywhere!" Lan snapped out of her weariness.

Hien put his head down, lip poked out in a show of hurt feelings. Lan wanted to slap herself. She cursed Han for making her this way. Lan swept Hien into a fierce embrace of her own. "I'm sorry little one, I'm sorry."

Hien melted into his mother's embrace. "You're sad." Hien wanted to cry for his mother.

"Yes!" Lan cried out, voice cracking in the same manner she was inside.

"Why?" Hien's question was innocent.

"I can't tell you!" Lan told him as she cried loudly. Crying into Hien's scalp, she was unable to tell him that his father wasn't the god he adored but the demon she feared.

***

Chapter Nine: October 24, 2007.

The aroma of Hollister's homemade *bánh cuốn,* traditional rolled rice pancakes wrapped in pork, perfumed the kitchen. Rosaline sat at the kitchen table, looking better today than she had in weeks in terms of her health. Her appetite and empty plate was proof. They managed to get through another week without a fainting episode.

He cleaned the empty dishes and glanced over his shoulder. The air around her felt like a mess. Her head was hung down. Any traces of their previous lively conversation had been replaced with tense silence.

He slid into a chair opposite her and folded his hands. "You don't have a next move, do you?"

Her eyes looked shiny and filled with fear. She shook her head and stared off in space.

Hollister sighed. "It's been a few weeks."

"I have nowhere to go. You've been doing all this stuff for me and I don't even know how to repay you."

He closed his eyes in thought. He had an idea but it was a crazy one for both of them.

"I think I can help."

"You can?" Her voice sounded more eager than she planned on it by the way she cleared her throat afterwards. "I mean, can you help me?"

He braced himself for his next words: "Marriage license."

Pearls of laughter erupted from his female guest. "Are you kidding?"

"Not if you don't have anywhere to live or anything to wear. And groceries cost."

"I've worn out my welcome." She scrambled to stand on her feet. "I get it."

He held a hand up. "I never said that."

"Just tell me when you want me out." That stubborn manner she trademarked crept back into the room. “I can leave tonight.”

"Not if you don't even have a means to get there. Impounded *stolen* car. I don’t think you’ll be doing a lot of walking either."

Rosaline folded her arms. "And that's your trump card over me? The fact that I can’t drive?"

He snatched off his shades in irritation and gave her a severe look. “Miss Welsh, this does not get me off. Sit down and shut up for a minute.”

Rosaline sat down into her chair, pouting and staring at the wooden floor like a child not getting her way. "You were saying?"

Hollister placed an authority in his voice. "Get a job and get it together. Maybe get some professional help. Keep yourself healthy. You need a routine, some stability."

“That’s not the part I’m having a problem with,” she wrinkled her nose, “The part *I’m* having a problem with is taking your last name.”

“I’m not demanding any wifely duties.” *Though I would not refuse them.* “This is a convenience thing only. You need a real ID. Someone else will figure out the current one you have is a fake.”

“You said get a *real* marriage license.”

“I don’t see any other Mrs. Lianos coming my way.”

“This is going to do what for me?”

“Help you hide.”

“You think I’m hiding from something —”

“I *know* you’re hiding from *someone*.”

“Whatever,” she scoffed.

“If you have a better idea, then please...”

“I can get a new ID on my own,” she insisted.

“Didn’t you say that the fire took all your known identifiers and possessions except your birth certificate?”

“Yeah and…”

“The redhead that doesn’t work definitely doesn’t eat.”

Rosaline tapped her foot against the tile furiously, “How do we do this then, smarty?”

“Use your real birth certificate and the fake driver’s license to get a real marriage license with me. Then use the real marriage license to get another social security card *and* a new ID. You’ll be Dana Liano only long enough to masquerade. We can make it look like someone stole your identity. I can even get someone to make up a police report.”

"You're serious," she gawked.

"As a heart attack."

"Who just signs their last name away like that?"

"Liano isn't my real name. So use it."

"Maybe I should get your *real* ID." Rosaline pointed a finger at him.

"Lucas is a credible enough threat. I get a feeling that *he's* the reason you're upset." *What is it you're not telling me?*

"I'm not going to pour out my soul every chance you come in the room."

"Look, I still have friends in the department. They can help. They can pull his background —"

Her hands shook as mistrust emanated from her even as she growled. "I suggest you leave it alone. I left town for my *own* reasons."

"You put quite a bit of distance between you and him." *I care enough about you*... Hollister wanted to shout these words but kept his cool.

Rosaline jumped out of her chair.

He managed to take her by the elbow before she could slip away. "Really, I just want to help."

"Maybe you should take your own advice." Rosaline pulled away before leaving the kitchen.

***

Chapter Ten: October 26, 2007:

Rosaline paced the living room. She wrung her hands, wiped her brow and mumbled things that were incoherent even to her ears. She would stare at her purse then shake her head followed by more pacing. Minutes later, she finally noticed someone standing in the kitchen.

"Hollister!" She pushed the joy out her voice, trying to play it cool. "Oh, you're home." She stood straighter. "Of course it was time for you to come home from work. I'll let you sleep."

"Are you okay?"

"Fine," she answered too quickly, "I'm fine."

Hollister shook his head in disagreement. "You're not fine."

"Save the reading my body language crap for another time. You *were* a detective, not now."

"You're walking a hole into my floor."

She stood still for a moment, muscles visibly tensed, before relaxing. "I'll be ready later."

He shrugged. "Okay."

"Marriage license," she gave him her best poker face, "I'll do it."

"Oh?"

She strained to detect any emotion in his voice. "I figured this would work better — for me."

He sounded casual. "Of course."

"I guess we should head out in a few after your nap, *honey*."

She felt his eyes running over her then heard the sarcasm loading his voice. "Sure thing, *love*,"

*

Their sham should not have been so easy. Yet, by the next week, "Dana Welsh" became "Dana R. Liano." Rosaline studied the documents in disbelief. The new driver's license gleamed under the light. Her new social security card would follow momentarily.

"All we did was shell out the money and flash my fake ID."

"Told you so."

She started at the marriage license. "So getting married was my dying wish?"

"According to your non-existent terminal disease, yes. I made up the dying thing for a sympathy play to get the clerk to move faster."

"Wow. I'll stop feeling bad about lying since you did enough of it for us."

"Besides, the dude pissed me off with how much he kept staring at your face." Hollister cut up her fake ID and discarded it. "So begins a new life, Mrs. Liano."

She wondered if she mourned for the loss of her lie more than the possibility of losing her life if Lucas found her. Rosaline hugged herself. "Should we toast our matrimony with a little champagne?"

"Just do me the honor of sleeping at night."

Lucas' crime forced her to abandon the only life she knew in south Florida. The complexity of being the alias Dana Cole collided with the newest deception of being Dana Liano. Each layer uncovered in one of those identities presented another layer to deal with— layers determined to strangle her.

Rosaline studied Hollister with the same critical eye she used with the photography. "Why are you helping me?"

She remembered the vulnerability she displayed in Hollister's embrace. What were *his* layers?

He closed the gap between them. She was inches from his face when he removed his sunglasses, his dark eyes shining. "I won't let the big bad wolf find you."

***

Chapter Eleven: November 2, 2007

Hollister sat at the monitoring station with all the colored monitors focused on different areas of the credit card company, watching for suspicious activity that seemed to never occur on his patrols. He absent-mindedly fingered a tiny silver cross under his collar during the shift tonight. A missionary gave Lan the tender relic during the secret meetings they were holding in a small village a few miles outside of Hanoi. Lan really believed that the God they preached about would save her and her son. Was being in America true salvation?

*

Lan swung the cross like a surrender flag while wildly pulling her son. Lan snuck out and took Hien with her. She left Han sprawled on the kitchen floor, soaked in beer from the bottle she hit him with. Lan fell at the feet of the American missionaries crying and spitting her native tongue so fast, even the most skilled translators of their group couldn't understand her mad ravings. A woman, pale and taller than the tiny Asian woman, took Hien into her arms as Lan cried and begged for Hien to be saved at least.

"I'll go anywhere, just take me! Take me, take my son! Take us to your god!" Lan pushed her son further into the arms of the woman with the hair colored like the sun, appealing to the paler lady as if she was a god that could save them.

A white man in a crisp American military uniform finally spoke to Lan in terse Vietnamese, taking her by the arm, "Lady, the people can't just take you two, we're trying to get these American citizens out of the conflict..."

The white soldier never got to finish that statement, since all of the sound in the world left Hien's ears… A restless remainder of the War followed. A crazed suicide bomber had taken the missionary's camp out, assuming that the holy people were an elaborate ruse for the Americans to continue screwing up their beloved Vietnam…

Hien woke up in an uncomfortable bed in a strange place, covered in bandages and the world was growing very dim to his sight… Hien asked the pale people for his mother for two weeks straight, until a male nurse had enough decency to answer him. The nurse communicated to the boy that too many dark-haired skinny women have already passed through the makeshift American military hospital already. They all looked alike. Young Hien communicated that this one was different, she was a butterfly. Then the white woman with the sunny hair came into the tent and placed the silver cross around Hien's neck. The sun-haired woman gently told Hien in her broken Vietnamese that his mother went to Heaven…

*

This latest memory forced him to bite into the sweaty fabric of his work uniform. He couldn't start crying and screaming in the bathroom at work. His concern should be wrapped up in Rosaline, his wife—no, he squeezed his eyes shut and counted to ten. She was just playing house with him. She wasn't *really* his wife.

Hollister swallowed hard. He had to see the therapist today before chickening out.

*

Later the next day, the business card directed Hollister to a blank office building starved of any true architecture. He glanced at the card again.

He didn't care about his feelings and definitely was not interested in talking about them. Hostile opposition welled up inside for him as he walked inside. Suite 212 looked so inviting inside, more furniture store than therapist's office. The three other nuts were trying to wait with him, bored by the magazines or by the standard cable news programs running in loop on the television. The brunette receptionist was too sunny for his taste. She flounced around in what may have passed as appropriate office attire here, but not anywhere else he knew of. At least Rosaline didn't have to place her sexiness on display; she could attract enough men with just her smile. Hearing his name called after a twenty minute wait prompted Hollister to want to leave but then a second door opened somewhere in the office. A tan-skinned woman in his age group appeared in a power suit and smart-looking reading glasses.

"Detective Liano?" The woman in the suit walked straight up to him.

Great, now the three other nuts knew he was a crazy cop. Hollister swallowed his anger. He stood up, shook the doctor's hand in a civil manner.

"Shall we?" Dr. Weathers pointed to the second door, waiting open for them to step through. The other side of his sanity, he imagined.

"I guess." *That sounded lame, Liano.*

Hollister followed her to a plush office colored in serene greens and blues, bookshelves neatly held materials for her eyes only. The setting was intimate with two chairs and a couch for the doctor near a coffee table. Psych magazines and a pitcher of water rested on the coffee table with an empty glass. Dr. Weathers offered Hollister a drink, which he gladly found to be a great stall as he poured himself a glass. They took their appropriate places and the doctor began speaking, her notepad out.

“I got your file from Dr. Winters in Tampa. You did not finish your psychological evaluation required for you to return to employment after a –”

Hollister cut her off, “I left Tampa. Too much attention.”

“On your own, of course?” Her voice sounded devoid of emotion.

“I’m a private person. I resigned and took a leave of absence.”

“You seem to care enough about what others think if you took time off.”

“My superior asked me to leave. Besides, I *like* what I do. It’s the only thing I *want to* do.” *It’s the only thing I can do* stood out in the back of his mind.

“Detective Liano, if you hope to return to work as a detective, then please answer my questions.” His whole being put up a wall that even the therapist felt.

“I’m not crazy,” Hollister mentally slapped himself for stating the obvious.

“Having your guard up doesn’t help me or you,” Dr. Weathers pointed out.

“What do you want to know? That I have an anger issue?”

“Do you, detective?” Dr. Weathers looked up in a curious manner.

“This is stupid,” Hollister grumbled, rubbing his temples. He was getting a headache. He took another sip of water to calm his nerves.

“I have to let the department know if you’re competent enough to serve again,” Dr. Weathers pointed out clearly.

Hollister dropped his words as heavily as he sat his glass on the table, “I killed him.”

Dr. Weathers sat there with her pen in her hand, taking notes. She kept her face neutral at his confession. "You said it was self-defense."

"The media doesn't care. He was an upper-class kiss up with a little power. He was free to do anything." Hollister wiped the sweat from his brow. Pieces of his memory began kicking around his head.

"When did you realize you shot the suspect?"

"When I saw blood!" He hit the table like a bullet.

Dr. Weathers continued to turn the verbal knife unflinching, "Detective Liano, another officer said you were there for several minutes over the suspect's body."

"I don't remember and I'm not *trying* to remember," Hollister rose to his feet. He was ready to leave.

The doctor took her smart glasses off, pinching the bridge of her nose in what appeared to be frustration, "Detective Liano, maybe you can grant me the privilege of being cooperative. Right now you are not doing a very good job at that."

He looked from the door back to her, then back to the door. He wanted to go back. The leave was only supposed to be for a year, maybe a year and a half. He stated the terms in his own letter.

Besides, he wanted to sleep free of guilt again and stop dreaming. He wanted to stop blacking out and doing things in anger that he couldn't take back.

He had an anger problem that needed to be dealt with. He sat back down, sighing hard.

Dr. Weathers took her pad back up, "Now tell me again what happened that night."

The dark-haired man willed himself for a battle in his own mind:

"I was responding to a call in Hyde Park, the nice side of town. A forty-year-old male barricaded his wife and son in a closet downstairs. A messy divorce as a motive. I get inside his house because I can't wait for SWAT. I tried to talk the guy down by the book to get a peaceful resolution out of this. Then the wife breaks out the closet. She's screaming, he's yelling. I'm trying to keep everything under control."

Hollister stopped for a moment to wet his throat with another drink from his glass. Dr. Weathers' pen was going as furiously as his words. "I hit the ground, weapon drawn. He shot her right in front of me with three rounds. He's foaming at the mouth and waving that revolver. Now it's lethal force. I tried to wrestle him down to the carpet. His son ran out after he heard the shot. The kid saw his own mom… He pointed it at the kid and I pointed my weapon."

"Detective," Dr. Weathers interrupted him. She stopped scribbling, "We can stop for today."

Hollister pulled himself from his memory. His hands were shaking and wet. It was too fresh of a memory to live with, even in a story. It was after four o'clock according to the clock. He wasn't back in Tampa. It wasn't July Seventeenth. His hands weren't bloody and he didn't have gun residue burning his fingers.

***

Chapter Twelve: November 3, 2007

Late Saturday afternoon Hollister pulled up outside the whitewashed antebellum home and left his cell phone on the passenger seat. He stepped onto the driveway as the ornate front door opened up to reveal Mother Myra Stone Hutchins. The elderly black woman wore gold-rimmed reading glasses and a jogging suit. He pictured a halo hanging over her silver hair.

"God is good, baby! Good enough to bring you near my way!"

Both she and the aroma of Southern cooking greeted him as he reached the door. The magnolias and marigolds in the massive flower garden swayed in welcome for his visit.

"Mrs. Hutchins, good to see you." Hollister gave her a faint smile then stepped inside.

"Stop being shy and hug me, I stopped biting a long time ago!"

He gave her the best hug he could muster up. Affection was still an art that eluded him.

Mother Hutchins studied him. "You look healthy. Still got them sunglasses, I see."

"They're prescription, Mrs. Hutchins, and you don't need to fuss over me like I'm one of your grandchildren."

"Stop that nonsense. You are like one of my grandchildren. Baby, you hungry?"

"I'll be lying if I said I wasn't. Everything smells wonderful!"

"Good! I can teach you something else to cook. Maybe if Leland learns a little of this, he'll get Jeanne to pay attention." Mother Hutchins pulled Hollister to the stove, sharing with him her secret to good collard greens and ox tails, as she stirred the simmering pot.

"No, I think they both pay attention to each other very well." Hollister had first noticed the romantic tension between tomboy Jeanne Roberts and skirt-chasing Leland Roland Brown when they were all study buddies taking criminal justice at USF.

Mother Hutchins poured another glass of iced tea for herself. "How are you, baby? What's going really on?"

Hollister chewed slower, trying to stall on rehashing the year. "With what, Mrs. Hutchins?"

"Well, life."

"Life's not bad."

"But it ain't great."

"I've had a long year," Hollister admitted after the rest of the cake disappeared in his mouth.

"I'm retired. What else am I going to do today?" she countered. "Leland said there was a lot of trouble surrounding you."

Hollister's voice begged her not to dig deeper. "Life isn't fair, Mrs. Hutchins, that's all. Some of us just get more of the crap."

"The hurt can't be that deep, deep enough that you can't forgive anyone or anything. Think about what you're saying."

He decided to change subjects this time. Rosaline's bruises came to mind. "I do have a question for you, Mrs. Hutchins"

"I'm listening."

"Why don't some people want help?"

"Maybe it depends on who they're asking for help."

"If I wanted to help someone who was in a bad situation –"

"Help is something people take when given to them. You can't force it on them."

"But I know that this person needs it more than they realize –" Hollister wanted to help Rosaline undo whatever evil had been forced upon her.

"God draws people to the healing waters, but you have to drink it."

Mother Hutchins leaned over the table, taking his face in her weathered hands. "Listen to me, Hollister. Don't be alone."

He wanted to bawl. Just like he did as a boy, when he hid in closets somewhere to escape the abuse surrounding him. He wanted to run, but felt like a larger presence arrested him. He sat fixed in his chair, listening to her talk.

"Don't punish yourself for what other people should have done for you. They should have loved you right and they didn't. *God is your help*, do you understand me, baby?"

He managed to gently break her hold, choking back the emotion produced in that rebuke from the church mother, "Yes."

"I'm praying for you, Hollister. *Don't* take that lightly."

*

The drive back to Jacksonville felt longer than his mind wanted it to. His thoughts crowded like the storm clouds gathering in the sky. *I'm not him, I'm not him.*

Halfway through the drive, his cell phone started singing. Hollister grabbed it at the first red light he reached. "Liano,"

"Hien?" The voice belonged to someone with a Midwestern twang to her speech.

"Mother," Hollister forgot to go once the light turned green, until a driver reminded him gently with a continuous car horn.

Hollister did not feel like this right now. Not driving, not on a Saturday, not on any other moment in time or place. "What is it, Mother?"

His voice began to match the impatience of the driver behind him.

"I'll make it short. Thanksgiving is coming up and I hope to see you."

"In Kansas?" His blood turned cold. He had no desire to see her. "Leland invited me—

"I understand, but you haven't been back for a few years and I'm sure Mrs. Hutchins would not mind if you had a little Midwestern cooking. I know Kenneth has been gone a few years and sometimes it's hard… but I'd really like for you to be here this year."

Hollister's heart tightened a little. He could hear the tears in Elizabeth's voice more than he pictured them. His adopted father, Kenneth Liano, died four years ago, around the same time Hollister stopped going back to Kansas for the holidays.

"I just moved to Jacksonville, Mother, I don't have a lot of money saved up –" Hollister checked the excuses he had on file in his memory bank.

"I can get you a ticket. I still have some of your father's old clients who are willing to be kind. You know money's never been a problem with us."

"Mother, the rain is coming down harder. I don't think this is a good time to talk." *Ever.*

Elizabeth continued in vain pleading with her son by adding memories, "The Jamersons will be there. Do you remember them? He was stationed in Hanoi near the missionaries I traveled with. Then there's that nice soldier who was in the MASH unit when you were recovering from the blast. He has family here. Oh and Mr. Adrian Hollister's daughter is stopping by. She's here to sell the Hollister home. I guess she felt as if she'd held on to it long enough. You do remember the nice college girl who spent her summers here?"

Hollister used half of the country to place distance between that life and him.

As if on cue, his adopted mother started talking, "I apologize for things being strained between us, Hollister. Can we just –?"

"Can I just call you back, Mother?"

"Of course. I'll be here when you want to talk. Good night, Hien – I mean, good night, Hollister."

*

The sky and the ground blended into a single color of gray that made driving more difficult after the rain came down. Hollister pulled into the driveway an hour later and got out of the car—only to be met by strong wind. He chased his trash can into the wet streets and got soaked in the downpour.

Once inside his house, he dripped water on the smooth tiles as he padded through the kitchen. Rosaline stood in front of the large picture window in his living room with her back to him. She made no indication she heard him.

Hollister headed to the bathroom to get out of the wet clothing before he caught a cold. He grabbed a towel off the rack then saw a glimpse of himself in the mirror looking drenched and pathetic…

The world felt so out of touch from his private hell.

***

Chapter Thirteen: November 11, 2007.

Rosaline stood in front of that picture window for hours. She'd had her mental health day, texting Lovely for a pick-me-up girly conversation and drowning sorrows into a large pint of French vanilla ice cream. She came to the realization that a light was on in the house.

Rosaline went toward its source.

Through the door-crack, she caught a glimpse of Hollister in his bathroom removing his shirt. She told herself to look away for privacy's sake but a nagging curiosity compelled her to keep watching. The mirror faced the door in his bathroom, but she couldn't see his face.

She choked.

Deep, finger thick long scars trailed their way down his spine. She couldn't recognize the normal instruments of abuse that would have placed such scars there – belts, extension cords, tree switches, shoes, hands.

It looks like someone beat him with a stick. A light came on in her mind. *Somebody beat Hollister.*

A common thread linked them. They had a vested interest because they shared scars.

The door flew all the way open. She covered her mouth.

His hard stare held an accusatory light inside of it. "Do you *ever mind your own business*?"

No answer followed from her.

The door slamming in her face couldn't even motivate her to move.

*

His bruises gnawed at her all week until she decided to ask him about them.

She slipped into his office to find him engaged in a pool game, studying the colored balls on the green top table intently. He didn't seem to notice her standing across from him as he lined up another shot to send the eight ball in the corner pocket.

Rosaline cleared her throat. "You can quit being the tough guy and just admit someone once made you cry, too."

Hollister scratched the table and missed his shot completely. He slammed a fist on the billiards table, spitting out some foreign words she wished she understood. "I was going to win."

Rosaline shrugged. "You're playing yourself. You win either way."

"*What* do you want?"

"I'm not the only one hiding baggage. It's not fair for me to be the messed up one when you're clearly messed up, too."

Hollister tossed the stick on the table. "You're trying my patience."

"You know my secret, so what's yours?" Rosaline found her boldness and walked up to him, "You said you were adopted, so you're not from here. Did your replacement parents try to beat the New World into you because they couldn't return to sender? Or were your blood people less than ideal? They'd rather beat the love out of you than give it? Ask me how I know, Liano."

Their face-off ended when Hollister brushed by her, slamming the door on his way out. Minutes later she heard his car peeling out the driveway.

*

She remained in the living room for thirty minutes, waiting for him to return then started down the hall toward his bedroom. Rosaline noticed that his bedroom in the back of the house was so—cool. Cool in the effect that it was painted in serene ocean blues.

The room had an ornate sleigh bed in the center and a matching dresser. Night stands of scented cedar were on each side of the bed. Blackout curtains draped the windows. He kept his closet neat and catalogued – shirts hung carefully on the left, pants on the right side. Everything was separated according to how casual it looked. She closed the closet and got on her hands and knees to look under his bed. A small lock box under the bed got her attention.

Rosaline reached for it and took a seat on the floor. A few Polaroid pictures, a kite, and a dog-eared black book made up the contents. The aged, yellow documents looked legal. Adoption papers she guessed. She tried working the foreign name around her tongue until someone snatched the papers from her.

Startled, Rosaline slid back into the nightstand.

Hollister leaned over her. "It's *Luu Hien,* and we need to redefine personal space." The electricity seemed to jump from his eyes. "Be happy I don't have my gun."

"You would shoot little old me?" She placed a hand on her bosom in melodramatic fashion.

The way his eyebrows jumped up from behind those sunglasses told Rosaline that maybe she should think twice before speaking again.

"You're just not content with being an annoyance? You have to come and break into my room?"

"How is it breaking and entering if I'm staying here, *detective*? You gotta agree with me, at least about the letter of the law."

"Get out," he demanded, standing to his full height.

"I saw your scars," Rosaline began softly. "Don't you think it's unfair if I'm the only one being honest? What makes your secret so dark and heavy it can't be handled? You need to earn my trust if you want it so badly."

Hollister swallowed, staring off in the distance. After several minutes, he stretched out on the floor, sitting down with his back resting against his bed frame.

Rosaline posed herself into an Indian-style seating. She pointed to the papers he had placed back in his box. "You're adopted."

"I didn't lie."

"Didn't your real parents want you?"

"I don't know, and I'd rather not go into it."

"It's funny when the shoe is on your foot, isn't it? You don't want to talk about it."

"I've seen a lot of victims of all types of abuse. It's in my nature to want to ask those types of questions. Especially when the abuse was… right in front of me," he said, referring to the night he changed her clothes. "You think I was bored or something?" He grew quiet. Painful seconds ticked by. "If I tell you this, you have to get off my case about it."

"What a funny thought—getting off someone's case when one doesn't want to talk about things."

Hollister seemed too tolerant of her sharp tongue, because he gave an answer to her burning question after another long pause. "Bamboo."

Rosaline's nose wrinkled up. "Like in China, bamboo?"

"I'm Vietnamese, close enough."

"Someone hit you with bamboo?" Rosaline hoped to fish the story.

"No, someone hit me *very hard* with bamboo," he corrected in a bitter way.

"Someone in your family?"

"It was someone close enough."

"Maybe that's why you were adopted."

"The bruises have nothing to do with it."

She noticed the quiet detective had a lit fuse lurking behind those shades. "Okay… didn't someone try to stop whoever hit you?"

He smirked in a grim manner. "Maybe God."

"You are – excuse me – you were a detective and you can't handle this line of questioning?"

"Easier said, I guess." He threw a hand up as if to dismiss the contradictions of his actions.

"Didn't they love you? Didn't they want to keep you?" Her heart slipped into her next question. "They're dead, Rosaline, and I came over here when I was ten. I'm thirty-two now." He took his shades off and covered his eyes …Was he crying? She forced herself to look down.

"Somebody told me that the death of a parent ages you."

"Your wisdom is very valuable, grasshopper," he mocked.

"My dad was in the hospital when he died…" She covered the bridge of her nose to hold her tears. "Cancer. I can't stand to be in hospitals now for anything."

"I'm sorry."

"I think you deserve it more than me—"

"I don't miss my father."

Rosaline looked up at him, her hair standing on end.

His next set of words rushed out from his lips like water freed from a dam. "My father bruised my backside like this. He told me," Hollister spoke in Vietnamese then translated, "That he'll beat out whatever Lan did to me to make me a sissy. He didn't make sissies."

Rosaline flinched like she was the one who took Hollister's punishment.

He continued with fists balled up. "Whatever hits I didn't take, my mother did. She jumped in front of my father one day to keep him from killing me with that stick. Then he turned on her like a rabid dog… what – what – what man beats the woman he claims to love? What – what type of bastard rapes his own wife in front of his kid to prove that *this is what a man is*?" Hollister stood to his feet. "I'm done."

Rosaline grabbed his sleeve. “She loved you enough to take your beatings.” No wonder he asked her those brutal questions. He saw it for himself on a very *personal* basis.

“Yeah, and what good did that do?”

“I know what that feels like. When – when you expect somebody or something to save you and they don’t. They just – just don’t. But they try, they do try.” Rosaline knew somewhere in her words, that statement was more for her benefit than his. Her father came to mind... Hollister must have forgotten to cover his emotions because his shades were still lying on the floor. His smooth yellowish-tan face looked so pained. She wanted to press more, disregarding whatever horrible consequences would follow. He pulled away, forcing her to land on the carpet. Rosaline pulled herself up to her knees, arms out as if begging for him to listen. Hollister left his own bedroom, forcing Rosaline to think that he was going to leave her alone.

Rosaline choked. They shared bruises and she did not want to be the only one dealing with it. She didn’t want him to be alone, either.

*

The bathroom was a hideous throw back to 1976. She was twelve, and the fact that she could bleed made her feel no more of a woman than sneaking halter tops to wear at school from her aunts’ closets. Rosaline had been so careful to not stain anything. She swiped those embarrassing girly things from the store; the aunties barely sustained her on a diet of grits and stale bread, so she didn’t expect them to care about her personal hygiene. When she stood up she saw the rust-colored stains mocking her on the fuzzy pink carpet of the bathroom floor.

Was it Monday yet, so she could go back to her father’s.

Grandmamma's stale house depressed her.

Grandmamma was a blanket term for the shriveled old woman who popped out her father. Maybe the old woman was pretty once. Rosaline figured that the four harpies called her aunts stole her Grandmamma's beauty from the womb.

Drama Auntie Tara banged on the bathroom door, yelling. "Hurry and move it! I need to pee like a racehorse."

"I got blood on the carpet," Rosaline admitted. Maybe the Drama Auntie Tara's heart would double in size today.

Drama Auntie Tara burst into the locked bathroom like a SWAT team on a drug deal in their neighborhood. Rosaline froze for a moment. The thick woman's face was transfigured into horror. "What did you do?"

"I got a period," Rosaline said, thinking that the Drama Auntie Tara would give her sisterhood and sympathy.

"On the carpet I bought for Mama!" Drama Auntie Tara gave a thrilling show of shock and awe, hand on her head as if agonizing over the few bucks she wasted in the discount store.

"It's ugly, anyway." Rosaline's smart mouth came from her mama, Lela Cole.

Drama Auntie Tara snatched her up by the collar of her t-shirt. "What did you say?"

"That hurts!"

"Answer me."

"It's ugly! The stupid carpet's ugly!"

"You little –!" Drama Auntie Tara's rage reached its crescendo.

Rosaline freed herself from the choke hold. "I want my daddy! I wanna go home!"

"He ain't your daddy. That's what Michael gets for feeling bad for Lela's whore-hopping."

"You just mad because your stupid daddy didn't want you!"

Drama Auntie Tara's lips twisted in a manner that scared Rosaline beyond understanding. She turned and disappeared from the bathroom. Rosaline studied her neck in the mirror. She didn't want the teachers asking her all their nosy questions about her home life.

Drama Auntie Tara descended upon Rosaline with the extension cord ripped from the wall. She peeled away the pink fabric on Rosaline's back to expose her flesh and started swinging. Rosaline screamed and tried to block the blows with her hands. That only gave Drama Auntie Tara more places to hit. The bathroom wasn't big enough to make an escape.

The other three harpies formed an audience. Divorced Auntie, Lazy Fat Auntie, and Boogie Auntie crowded the door calmly as Drama Auntie Tara continued to beat Rosaline. None of the women tried to stop it. Their abuse of Rosaline was a normal activity, like doing hair and smoking cigarettes.

Divorced Auntie Sara spoke. "Tara, whoop that mouthy girl later. We gotta go by Sam's. I need to get my curlers to do Candy's hair."

"Whup that little heifer! She ate my Twinkles." Fat Lazy Auntie Cookie cheered the beating on.

Boogie Auntie Candy yawned. "Sara needs to do my hair and the curlers are at Sam's! I even waited three dates before I went up to his penthouse! Cookie, you ate your last Twinkie, fatso!"

More commotion in the hallway followed until a tall black man shoved his way into the bathroom. He began yelling, pulling Drama Auntie Tara back. "Get off of her, Tara! She's only twelve!"

Rosaline saw her angel reaching out to her. Michael Welsh pulled the crying, bruised girl into his muscular arms. He cradled Rosaline like a baby. "Tara, what is wrong with you!"

"I'll kill her!" Drama Auntie Tara screamed, swinging the extension cord with promise.

"Move, all of you!" Michael demanded, pushing his way through the house. The women began following Michael like a cloud, pouring out their grievances concerning Rosaline.

Grandmamma tried to block the front door. "Son, don't cut me and your sisters off please."

Michael shoved his way out of the door as he carried his child. "If you can't accept her, you can't accept me! I'm through with all of you!" He placed Rosaline in the old Ford truck and sped off. He returned to the Welsh home as a memory after his untimely death. And even though he saved his daughter from the aunts' abuse, Rosaline would learn that her father didn't save her as she got older.

Lucas became the aunties' replacement.

*

Hollister froze after he saw her in the kitchen.

Rosaline told herself to keep her post at his kitchen table until he came home.

He still had on the same jeans and collared shirt from the night before. He stood there, staring at her, his mouth twitched and muscles flexed. He turned to leave the room. Moving with the speed of an officer in pursuit, she blocked his path of escape from his kitchen. Hollister grabbed the nearest wall to steady himself. His nostrils flared as he snapped. "We've been through this –"

Rosaline reached out, putting her hand on his shoulder. She felt him pull away, yet his feet stayed rooted in his spot. She wished he would confide in her like a husband would. She scolded herself for wanting to touch his face, scolded herself for standing so close...

"My aunts used to hurt me. Lucas hurt me. I'm so used to people hurting me. I don't know what it's like to breathe," she told him quietly. "You told me before that I wanted someone to know how Lucas hurt me. I want you to know these things because I know *you don't want to be alone with your pain either*. Please, just tell me *anything*."

He removed her hand, backing away. "I gave you an inch, don't take a mile."

***

Chapter Fourteen: November 25, 2007.

"Just tell me anything."

Anything?

Anything involved telling her he still cried in his sleep, still screamed in his nightmares, still cowered at the invisible blows given by his father. He could still hear his mother scream as Han pinned her down to the dirty kitchen floor and begged for him not to shame her in front of their own son…

He wanted to tell her *anything,* to see the quiet look in her eyes promising patience and understanding. Hollister was a detective, an EMT, a life-saver. He thought that nobody needed to save him, even as he drowned in his painful memories. The reason why he left the kitchen stood out on the edge of his mind: He grew sick with the revelation that he needed Rosaline as much as she needed him.

His past had been exposed. Somehow, the good Lord thought it would make great sport to send a woman with a similar broken spirit his way to see if they could fix each other.

*

He watched Rosaline wiping away stray tears as she stood in the bathroom.

He knew he was too raw to deal with anybody right now. *She* needed someone to be strong for her, but he felt too weak to even qualify. *He* wanted to be the strong one. He hated whatever sissy qualities Han Luu so badly wanted to beat out of him.

Now she wasn't just under his skin, she had wormed her way between his heartbeats. Hollister longed to hold her like he did the last time. He forced himself back into the safety of his bedroom, not waiting to give her wind that he had returned to the house. The work week helped him ward off the risk of connecting emotionally. Pouring out his heart to Rosaline meant crawling up into the gentle cradle of her reassuring words and soft touches.

You broke down. You're not strong, his mind reminded him.

He had been seeing the therapist. *He* was the one not admitting to his own problems. *He* was the harsh judgmental one. *He was wrong*. He hung his head down, sinking on the sleigh bed.

*

Dr. Weathers looked at Hollister with genuine concern during his next session. "Detective Liano, wanting to walk out of every session at the mention of your childhood is not healthy."

"What does that have to do with me getting my badge back, doctor?"

"Your childhood may provide a reason as to why you respond the way you do to nurture."

"Classic broken childhood. I feel better now. You've solved all of my problems, Doc. I do apologize for not talking to my inner child enough," Hollister answered with biting wit.

"My job is to determine whether or not you are competent enough to perform the duties asked of you, but all I'm seeing is that your past dictates a lot of your decision-making."

"And how many years of school did you take to get that one?"

"The shooting, detective, is a good example."

"That decision was independent of my life."

"Why did you become a detective?" Dr. Weathers asked him in a controlled tone.

"To help people. There's no deep psycho-babble behind it."

"Do you think people helped you in your life when you were younger? Maybe you felt as if no one was there or that no one understood any of the issues you had to deal with." Hollister couldn't follow up with a witticism after those words. She dug deeper. "Was there any type of abuse or neglect in your family?"

"Elizabeth and Kenneth never touched me. They were just too stupid to know how to relate to me. The divorce made me their football."

"I recall you saying that you were adopted."

"I don't advertise it. You asked about my last name, and I explained it."

"Why were you adopted?"

"Some white woman thought it'd be chic to take a half-blind yellow kid from the wild jungle."

"You don't identify with your adopted parents. I see."

"How could I? They're not my real parents."

"What about your real parents? Why were you no longer with them?"

"I'll be generous and keep my smart comments to myself, but lay off the real parents slant."

*

His shooting had been publicized for weeks in Tampa. He learned to dislike the local media, especially the reporter dating his best friend, Keisha Green. Miss Green proved to be persistent in her quest for truth. He had to learn different routes to get back to the condo to avoid her. Even with Jeanne providing damage control, his name somehow leaked out to the right people with the right listening ears. The damage was done and Jeanne asked for his resignation.

His mind went back to their heated conversation:

He sat in the office, stunned by the request. "Why?"

"I have to make an example," Jeanne answered his query in her office, overflowing with paperwork and file boxes, "Unfortunately, you're it."

"And you can't do it with James?"

"I don't have enough evidence to do so," Detective Roberts tightly admitted, "He has some serious minded criminal friends who don't want to end their little partnership."

"That's not it. It's because I'm convenient. I'm the one whose name got out. Forget the fact that I've put my time in, did everything right..."

"Detective Liano..."Jeanne looked worn out by his arguing.

"Now it's Detective Liano." His hostile nature grew with every word from Jeanne.

Jeanne slammed his file down on her desk, staring at him with open annoyance. "I'm your superior, Hollister, so don't try to mince words with me. I'm asking you to leave. I can't have everyone in the department get burnt. I'm also trying to save you some face. Take some time off until this is cleared up. That's how we'll play it – that you're repentant enough over the shooting to resign. Go to therapy. Dr. Winters has other colleagues in other cities –"

"No, you want me gone until your good image is back."

"This is not about me. This is about you leaving the department in a proper fashion."

"James made you look like a fool. He was the bad guy all along."

"I don't make my vendettas personal enough that they cross into my professional life, detective. I think you would know more about that than I would."

Hollister ignored that blow to his psyche. "James embarrasses the department by blatantly taking a dealer's bribe, and I'm being asked to leave because of a mistake."

"Hollister, judging by what you told Leland, it doesn't sound like a mistake."

He took a deep breath. "And you're going to use that against me."

"You're getting unstable. Add the fact that you've already spent time in a cell in your own station. I have to do something. You're a ticking time bomb, and Heaven help whoever is in the way when you blow up."

"Jeanne, you know this isn't the right way to handle this. You know what that was about."

Jeanne did not address the latter statement. "I have the captain on my butt, waiting for me to make a decision! The longer you stay here as a detective, the worse it will get."

"Says who?"

"Says the internal probe I have to conduct in my entire narcotics unit until I find out who else is taking deals, looking the other way, killing innocent high school kids…" Jeanne stopped herself briefly. "I'm only saying it once — resign or I'll have to let you go for reasons I'd rather not justify. You already look guilty. Desperate people like James don't mind using scapegoats when available."

Hollister felt his stomach drop to his feet. "You aren't telling me something."

"I want the letter on my desk Monday morning. Unless you want to stick around long enough to see what else one scorned former detective can do to another."

Lashing out against one of his good friends was not going to help the situation. Hollister made the painful decision to end his career as a major case detective that Saturday night in August. Hollister ran a hand through his spiky locks, sighing at the sadness of his memory. Lashing out against Rosaline would not help him get back to that soft place of just being Hien.

*

A few days later, between trying to stay awake and trying to do work, Hollister gave Leland a call. The two men discussed life briefly before Hollister asked about a case he'd been working on.

His friend sounded more worn out than him. "This rabbit hole is getting too deep, even for me."

"Well, what's up?"

"I'll put it like this: Our friend has a friend, too."

“Reynolds?”

“Yeah, James and some small-time dealer had been really friendly. Some cat running errands for the Young Lordz.”

Hollister remembered that a case involving the violent gang had absorbed Detective Brown’s career for the last year. The Young Lordz had been developing dangerous connections to Columbia. Hollister’s last days in narcotics became volatile with these colorful characters. “Them again?”

“Yeah, I’m going through the case files at the desk right now. Most of major crimes’ resources are sunk into this one case. My C.I. just told me there’s a snitch in the group. Somebody didn’t get the memo to keep quiet.”

“Your snitch wants to cut a deal or something?”

“No, he wants big time. He approached another undercover about it. Says he has major leverage.” The sound of Leland furiously typing at his computer at his desk in the department carried to Hollister’s ear. He pictured Leland’s cell phone cradled between his ear and shoulder.

“What’s that peon’s name . . .? Kane? Kleane? Keane?”

Hollister’s ears snapped into attention, “Keane, Lucas Keane.”

“Yeah — yeah! I wrote it down on a piece of paper so I would put it in.”

“Run that name, Leland,” he demanded in a tense voice.

“You sound like you know something.”

Hollister let Rosaline's face flash across his mind as he cleared his throat, "It's come up before with me. Run that name fast, it might help you."

"I'll do that," Leland sighed over the phone, "I do not like where all of this will end. This department is under a serious magnifying lens, Hollister, and we're the little ants about to meet the burning laser of sunlight," Leland sounded more relaxed now, "You're sleeping must be off. I called the other day and you missed my call all together."

"I'm trying to get my body schedule back on track. I'll come straight back here tonight. Rosaline's going out after work." The mention of her name sent Hollister back to that funny, overprotective place he constantly found himself as of late. A place where the black and white perverted into a gray haze he couldn't navigate his logical mind through.

"Do you think that your… uhhh, roommate, will pick the phone up?"

Hollister groaned. "She is not my roommate."

"If she's not your roommate, then what is she?" Leland asked the question openly that Hollister had been asking himself inwardly. A pause interrupted the flow of their conversation.

"She's just someone staying with me." *Get off it.*

"Hollister, you're good, because if any woman that sounded that fine stayed with me —"

"Good night, detective," Hollister quickly ended the phone call, not ready for his carnal mind to chase that rabbit again. Not now. Hopefully, not ever.

Chapter Fifteen: December 22, 2007

Rosaline burst into Hollister's bedroom, singing of victory. "Guess who's keeping her temporary photography gig after the Christmas season? The store loves my shots so much, they're going to hire me on—" A suitcase and a pile of folded clothing caught her eye. "Did I miss something?"

Hollister gave orders as usual: "I need to be at JIA by six am to catch my flight to Kansas. You're driving."

An unfamiliar pain hit her heart. "Kansas? Why – why are you going to Kansas?"

"To right a wrong, I hope," he said in his mysterious manner.

Uncomfortable with the way she was responding to this news, she looked at the carpet. He owed her no explanations about what *he* did in *his* life.

"Hollister, I don't know. Being in your house alone..."

"You've lived here this long. Why sweat it now?" Hollister actually sounded surprised. "If safety is the issue, I can give you a temp security code, let someone at work I trust drive by here. I'll even call you if you'd like."

Her safety. Rosaline scoffed. Hollister was still thinking like a cop.

She wanted to beg him to stay, beg him to take her along, and throw herself in his luggage.

Instead, she told him good night so she could rest up.

*

Rosaline dropped Hollister off at the airport a few days after Christmas.

He only brought his duffel bag and a second carry-on piece of luggage to travel with. "Try to keep the wild parties to a minimum, will ya?" he joked in the departure lane.

"I guess have a nice flight, Supercop." Rosaline wore her sunglasses to hide the distress in her eyes at his leaving.

Hollister shut the door to get checked in, leaving her with a smile on his lips.

A yawning chasm of loneliness opened from deep within her.

Her personal safety wasn't the only issue, but she couldn't place into words why she got so upset.

*

Rosaline stood in front of the picture window on New Year Eve's night. There was only so much television watching she could do before she cracked. Rosaline sighed loudly. Hollister was freezing his little behind off somewhere in the Heartland, and she wanted to be a part of that. She stomped her foot like a little kid. His plans didn't involve her.

Her cell phone started singing from somewhere in the house. Rosaline raced out of the living room to find it in the bathroom by the sink. Rosaline squealed in delight when she saw the missed call was from Lovely Harrington.

After two rings, Lovely picked up. "Hello?" Her voice had an annoyed tone to it.

"Lovely!" Rosaline wondered if she sounded too overjoyed.

Lovely lost some of her edge. “Rosy Raz... dang, you sound bored.”

Rosaline took a seat on the edge of the tub. “I’m about to climb the walls.” Another thought came to her. “Wait. It’s New Year’s Eve and you called me? *You* might be the bored one.”

“I would have been in Atlanta partying by now, but I’m stuck in some stupid hick town trying to get my tire fixed...” Rosaline could hear Lovely berating someone she deemed incompetent at fixing her silver Jaguar. “It’s about time you got the right size tire. Are you even qualified to breathe near this very valuable piece of luxury? Maybe your paycheck is worth my tire!”

“I see the Jag gotta flat.” Rosaline hoped to ground Lovely before she flew off the handle. Having rich parents put Lovely in the clouds, not in reality.

“The rental Jag has a flat. You’re crazy if you think I’d put my baby on the highway! And with good reason! I figured Jacksonville was a big city—”

“You’re in Jacksonville?” Rosaline nearly fell backwards into the tub.

“Unfortunately.” Lovely would have sounded more thrilled about a root canal.

“Oooh, ooh!” Rosaline raced off to the guest room, tossing clothing aside and hunting for a pen. “Where are you? What road? What landmarks?”

“Some stupid place called Oceanway.” Lovely could only muster disgust.

Rosaline asked Lovely to get the mechanic to give her some directions. Her friend sounded confused but obliged. “Why do you want directions? I don’t even know where you are—”

“I’ll be there in thirty minutes.” Rosaline hung up then started digging through her make-up bag. If she timed it right, Rosaline could cut her usual beauty rituals into half and see her best friend.

*

The New Year came in with a bang. Rosaline rescued a rattled Lovely and swept her off into the magic of late-night Jacksonville. They danced like flames in the crowded club until Lovely pulled Rosaline off the floor for a sudden craving of greasy spoon fare. They chattered lively until the subject of Rosaline's whereabouts rolled around.

"Jacksonville all this time, huh?" Lovely's weak smile indicated some hurt behind the gesture.

Rosaline felt a gush of stories rush to her lips to reveal everything: Hollister, Tanda, Lucas, her fake marriage, being alone. But, being vague was a better solution, necessary for her friend's protection. "I regret not telling you about Jacksonville sooner."

"So for a few months you've been what – homeless? You're driving and you look too clean."

"I'm getting on my feet. That's what the guy I'm staying with suggested—"

"You live with a guy?" Lovely looked part-judgmental, part-amused.

"A quiet guy. He works at night, overly neat, cooks. Dresses like my old math teacher most days... and he's got all of his shots from the vet. What's up with the eye-rolling?"

Lovely held her fist up. "More power to 'ya."

"Thanks for mocking me."

"Now, if one of you doesn't make a move –"

Rosaline felt her color go to her feet. "He *never* touched me."

"He's gay," Lovely declared.

"He likes women!"

"There's only one of two ways you would know—"

"I just do!"

"Two straight people don't live together and something isn't going on. I'm just saying."

"We do."

"All right, all right, at least he's not the prick!"

Rosaline stepped her anger down to breathe. "No. This guy's not."

Lovely proposed a toast with their glasses. "Look, let's kiss and make-up. Cheers?"

Rosaline touched glasses graciously. "That Hypnotiq you drank must have you under a mean spell. You need to sleep that off." This comment drew the much needed laughter from the ladies.

"Girl, you were dancing like you've been locked away in a tower, let down your fiery red hair down more." Lovely snapped her fingers as if moving on the dance floor.

"I haven't done anything really fun in months. Eat, sleep, snap pictures for a paycheck, repeat."

"I miss my photographer." Lovely's words felt warm as the fur she was wearing. "When are you coming back?"

Rosaline stopped for a moment. She wanted that part of the state to become unrecognizable. Jacksonville had given her something new. "I don't know." It was a safe answer.

The heavy talk went down with the ice in their glasses. Lovely resumed conversation, weaving the magic needed to allow Rosaline to forget what the past year had bought her.

*

On the first day of the New Year, Rosaline woke up in an unfamiliar room by herself.

Sleepy-eyed, she flipped over in the bed to find a handwritten note on the dresser.

Headed to Hotlanta. Enjoy the rest of your stay.

Did I mention there was a hot tub in the bathroom.

-Love

She hugged her pillow and grinned. For one day, she could pretend to be problem free and slipped back into a nice sleep…

The bright sunshine of the late afternoon burst through the hotel windows, making her climb out of bed to find the toilet and that hot tub. The hot tub lived up to her expectations and she remained in the water until her skin pruned. Rosaline parted with the relaxing water and slipped in a terry cloth robe as soft as a kiss. She climbed into the bed then reached for her purse. The pictures from the club last night came to mind.

At the club, Lovely had complained in her drunken state that all Rosaline wanted to do was snap shots instead of live life. Rosaline made sure to capture parts of her living it up on New Year's Eve, the first photo being of Lovely giving a raspberry courtesy of a strong drink. Laughter rocked her hard enough to almost hit the floor. More digital shots of the two women dancing and goofing off filled the next series of shots. It was nice to have someone equalize the negatives of life with a few positives…until she ran across the picture that made her run away from Lucas.

*

Rosaline punched the NEXT button for ten minutes straight. Several shots of a young black man lying face down in a grassy field filled the tiny screen. Three bullet holes inside his chest stood out in the close up shots. There were face shots, close up, wide angles, side views of the body.... Then a white man came into view wearing a malevolent grin hiding some secret she did not want to know as he stood over the body with a .38 special.

The very last shot on her memory card had a smug Lucas Keane holding up a business card to the camera that read:

James Reynolds

Lead Detective, Narcotics, Tampa P.D.

Rosaline felt hands shaking. Bile collected in her belly. She had known about one of the evil snapshots. Not this many. Her memory card had been full of them all this time.

She scrambled off the bed and ran to the toilet.

Her mind went running in all directions as she rocked herself back and forth on the floor. The stale taste of vomit polluted her mouth.

Why did Lucas stop to capture the beauty of a bullet hole instead of the white sands of a lush waterway? He could rape her, but why rape her creative work?

The light bulb in her mind turned on: Lucas had sold many of her possessions for drug money, including the digital camera she had with her. After two weeks of searching, she paid an outrageous price to get it back from a low-end pawn shop in midtown St. Petersburg.

Maybe that's why he torched the house. He knew I got my camera back.

Her ringing cell phone made her jump several feet in the air.

Just like in a scary movie.

But this was no movie. She ran back to her purse to find the phone then picked up. “Hel-hello?” Maybe normalcy would come back to her voice.

“It’s five in the evening here in Topeka, my normal waking time on the East coast.” A familiar male voice came to her ears.

“Hollister?” Her heart leaped with joy she didn’t want to admit to.

“You don’t sound all there. Is everything okay?”

“I’m fine,” she blurted out.

“Are you sure? If you want to talk, I’ll listen.”

Rosaline touched her lips briefly, “Something didn’t agree with me. I just got – got sick.”

“I’m sorry to hear that. Do you need me to do anything?”

She sat on the bed. Even in another state, she noticed he was in cop mode. “No, just—Lovely got stuck in town and we went off clubbing. Just can’t hang like I used to.”

“Did you sleep at all?

Rosaline shot down the desire to beg Hollister to come back to Jacksonville and be in this hotel room so she wouldn’t have these thoughts of Lucas and dead people. “Don’t worry about me.”

“When you sound weird like that, how can I not be?” He paused. “Is it the piece of paper thing?”

"The marriage license?"

"Yeah."

"Hollister, that's settled. Really, I'm okay. How are you?"

"Surviving." He sighed. "Really, are you thinking about your ex?"

She didn't immediately answer.

"I'm sorry for being too forward after everything –"

"No! Of course not!" Her voice softened. "I'm just – just missing having my girl here. You didn't offend me." *I wish you were here.*

"Glad you weren't alone, I just wanted to be polite and say Happy New Year."

"I'm glad you went to see your adoptive mother, Hollister." Rosaline covered her mouth. "I'm sorry. That's none of my business."

"You figured out I went to see her."

"You said Kansas." Rosaline's nervous mouth continued to go on and on, welcoming the change of subject. "Just be glad you had a family and weren't the throw-away foster kid. A dysfunctional home feels better than none."

"Not all of us have the option of being raised by wolves."

"I'm sorry... I must still be messed up... " Rosaline threw in an apology, hoping to keep him on the phone longer.

"Water under the bridge again, so much it's an ocean. We're okay."

I'm not okay.

She wanted to tell him everything, but irrational thoughts cornered her: Surely he had friends in the department willing to help a half-crazed photographer unburden herself of such dangerous knowledge—unless there was a reason why she could not trust him. Would Hollister hide anything from her? He wasn't very forward about why he wasn't a cop anymore. Had Lucas ever crossed Hollister's path? Did Hollister know about the murder? Had he committed one? She knew he went to therapy for past problems…

Hollister cleared his throat and pulled her back to reality. "I have an afternoon flight that comes in tomorrow. Granted there isn't a delay, of course. Unless you really miss me, *honey,* and I'll hurry home to you tonight."

Rosaline pressed her lips tight together and chided herself internally. "Go fly a kite, Liano."

"Your concern touches me." He hung up following his last verbal jab.

She fell onto the bed, too scared to doze off.

Too many thoughts rush through her mind like cars on the highway.

*

The planes landing and taking off at the airport held Rosaline's photographic interest until she saw the familiar squared-framed sunglasses belonging to Hollister. He looked hip in his heavy Southpole jacket, jeans and Timberland boots. He scanned the crowd to find her waiting in her black jeans and faux leather black coat and headed toward her with his luggage.

The urge to leap into Hollister's arms and tell him about the pictures and how scary it was to be without him was strong. She shook herself. "You don't look like Mr. Evans today."

He studied his outfit. "Gotta stay warm." Then it seemed he was studying her. "You all right?"

"Now that you're back, *dear*, my world is complete."

"Oh, I couldn't sleep another wink without your lovely presence," He gave her a sarcastic smile then held out his hand. "Cough up the keys."

Rosaline dropped them into his open palm as she led him to his car.

She resolved to treat those pictures the same way Hollister treated his adoption papers—lock them up in a safe place and simply forget they existed. She could just press erase and make them disappear—but the tug-of-war between doing it and holding on to them kept her in limbo.

She didn't need to make a decision just yet.

***

Chapter Sixteen: January 21, 2008.

As Hollister walked by the bathroom in his home, the off-key singing flowing from the shower served him notice – he had missed Rosaline while he was in Topeka. Hollister struggled to put that thought out his mind while walking to his bedroom. Seeing the orderly state of the room ushered in a feeling of familiarity he needed. Hollister climbed into bed and stared at the ceiling, hoping sleep would soon follow. The time change and playing the polite son during the holiday had taken a toll on him.

He closed his eyes.

Even thousands of miles away, a certain redhead had crowded his thoughts. It felt like his body went to Kansas, but the rest of him remained behind in Jacksonville.

Hollister turned in the bed and clutched a pillow tight to his chest. If only *she* was the pillow instead… Come tomorrow, they would be just two people sharing a house with their lives crossing over at dinnertime.

Deep down, Hollister wished it was not this way.

*

The weekend before Single Awareness' Day, as Rosaline lovingly called Valentine's Day, they went to the mall to escape their routine and catch an action flick soaked in violence. After the movie, they hit the mall to walk around. They passed a jewelry counter.

Rosaline spun around. "Did I just see dangle earrings?"

He groaned inside. “Do we have to stop here?”

She seemed lost in her own world while gazing at a few expensive pieces on display.

“Ohh, pretty.” She tapped on the glass then called his name. “Look at this cute necklace.”

Hollister shook his head and approached the display case as requested. Rosaline pointed at a ruby necklace, her face fixed on the shiny piece.

The bored salesgirl took the cue. She looked more than eager to help them spend money. “Want to try it on?”

Rosaline nodded and the salesgirl carefully took the necklace from the case.

Hollister watched Rosaline fumble with the clasp for so long until it annoyed him. He turned to her and gave orders like he was a beat cop making an arrest. “Give me that.” He took the necklace out of her fingers and opened the clasp. “Now stand still.”

She made a face, but followed his instructions and placed her hands at her sides.

Hollister slipped the cool metal around her neck. “Okay, look up.”

Both of them studied the results in a mirror. Her face illuminated. “Wow.” Rosaline started making model-like poses in the mirror. “I love it.”

He didn’t want to admit that the necklace looked impressive on her, yet the words slipped out. “The white gold compliments your skin tone well.” The way the jeweler’s mirror showed her reflection, the light seemed to wink at Hollister as though it guessed his more secret thoughts about her beauty.

She clasped her hands together in joy. “Really? You think it looks good on me?”

“Very nice. Classy even.” He wasn’t sure if he answered her about how the necklace looked or how nice she looked with the necklace.

Rosaline sighed. “Okay, you can give it back to the nice sales lady. I’m done playing dress up.”

Hollister removed the necklace with shaky fingers, not sure why his control began to slip. All he did was put a necklace around her neck. He didn’t undress her. He made himself join reality, catching the disappointed looks on both women’s faces. The price tag wasn’t too heavy, but when one is on a budget...

Rosaline gave the sales girl a sad smile. “Thank you, miss.” Then, she cleared her throat and faced him. “Let’s find the food court and I’ll get you an iced coffee. My treat.”

“Sounds good.” They turned to leave. Hollister placed a hand on the small of her back—and snatched it back like he had been burned by fire. “I’m sorry.”

She stopped in the busy mall to give him a funny look. “What’s wrong?”

Embarrassment danced across his face as he held his hands up in guilt. “I’m sorry. My hand...”

“Oh.” Rosaline gave him a gentle smile. “I was wondering if I should’ve been worried about that salesgirl.”

A barrage of Vietnamese curse words raced across his brain. “I never want to disrespect you.” He cursed again. “That sounded so fake and forced. I’m—”

Rosaline laughed. “It was an accident. I understand.” She resumed walking then stopped again. “Besides, you don’t know that I know judo.”

“Judo?” Hollister cautiously walked up next to her. She was capable of violence he noted.

“Yeah, “ju” don’t know if I got a .38 in my purse.”

Hollister realized her joke was an attempt to break the weird tension he created. They resumed their journey to the food court. He made sure he walked with his hands buried deep in his slacks’ pockets.

The container of his restraint had already been turned over too many times.

***

Chapter Seventeen: March 8, 2008

The sound of keys jingling made Rosaline's heart swell as she slipped her early morning coffee. Hollister had just home from his overnight shift and she had an hour left before she went to the photo studio.

She tried to appear disinterested as he tossed his things in the living room and walked into the kitchen. He grunted a "good morning" then dropped a colorful card on the kitchen table.

"Was that?"

"Some invite I got in the mail for a block party." Hollister sounded like he was describing the mating habits of the tsetse fly as he went to the cabinet.

"A party!" Rosaline snatched the card up from the table, devouring its words. Her joy at the thought of attending filled her more than the breakfast bagel. "We get to go?"

Hollister kept his back to her as he poured himself a glass of water.

"Tell me you're going." The plea was visible in her voice.

"I don't do..." he began slowly.

"Anything! Don't you go crazy staring at the walls here?"

"You don't understand," His voice darkened.

“Then help me understand! It’s a party. It’s not the end of your life,” she insisted, throwing her hands up. She didn’t want to be alone at a party.

Hollister slammed his half-finished glass down in the sink, looking back at her.

His body language suggested a weariness not just produced by hard hours on the job.

*

Like flowers flourishing in the rain, Rosaline flourished in the festive atmosphere.

The people hosting the block party were a power couple made up of a white physician assistant and his Brazilian imported wife who loved tropical lipsticks and cha-cha heels. The cul-de-sac had been blocked off for parking as the couple’s backyard filled with chirpy partygoers. Spanish-style finger foods, a Latin DJ, and colored lights decorated the evening. Half-an-hour later, Rosaline and her hostess abandoned the men in search of the dance floor. A few hours later at the punch bowl, Rosaline saw Supercop making polite conversation with a group of other men. She caught his attention and waved at him from her position at the punch bowl... producing a funny expression on his framed face that seemed to get everyone else’s attention. *We are supposed to be married.* She winked back at him, laughing at how shy her “husband” truly was... A gasp later and Rosaline wasted her punch on the end of the table.

She saw Lucas standing next to her.

*

Her imagination was powerful enough to make her believe that her devil of an ex snaked his way into a city he didn’t even know she had gone to. Rosaline mopped up her mess up and realized this man was a look-alike. A wave haircut wearing, FUBU-sporting, lanky black man with Lucas' cocoa complexion was a look alike.

Mr. FUBU was smiling at her so hard it hurt, "Hi."

A picture of a snake charmer from the science channel popped into mind, leaving Rosaline to ask whether she was the one charming or was she being charmed.

"Hi." Rosaline tossed her pile of red-stained napkins into the trash bin near the punch table. She gave him the "bored shoulder." The "bored shoulder" was genetic in any woman who navigated environments made up of loud music and cover charges.

His forced charm was louder than the music. He cleared his throat, "You're too bright to be alone out here, black butterfly."

He was licking his lips as he rubbed his hands together. Did he intend to see her served up on the platter in the center of the food table? She cursed herself for buying the red-and-black number on the clearance rack with roses printed all over it and the exposed back.

"I'm not alone," she answered in a tone that would sink a stake into a coffin.

"Oh?" Mr. FUBU sounded both annoyed and intrigued. Rosaline wished her scaly skin would have scared him off. It might have been nice to have a disfigured face... "And who would let you flutter off?"

"Shouldn't you be in your cage? I'm not sure if you want my number or want to bite me. Neither one interests me."

Mr. FUBU grabbed her free arm before she could escape. "You might like that."

Lucas had said something to her like that in downtown St. Pete. Rosaline fixed him with a gaze that screamed "back off," she pulled away. "You *wish* you could find out."

Walking away, hips swinging, Rosaline felt powerful. No phone numbers scribbled on a cocktail napkin. Just her going to the dance floor. Mr. FUBU appeared in front of her.

Rosaline halted. "What is it that you *do* besides block me from the dance floor?"

He was quite full of his bravado, inches from her face, "I can do anything you want me to do but most people know me as a handyman."

He almost had her backing into the food table. She managed to duck him with a quick sidestep, "And I'm sure that comes in *handy*, excuse me." When she felt something tugging at her arm this time, Rosaline spun around violently enough to throw a punch. "*Look*, I said...!"

"Is everything okay?" Hollister stepped out of the darkness somewhere and came to her aid like a sentinel. He had her by the elbow. Some of his attention focused on her, but some of it focused somewhere else.

The "somewhere else" brazenly walked up to both of them, clearly ticked. "Hey man, uh – you're interrupting me and the lady."

Now the FUBU snake seemed rustled that another male had entered his territory. What was she, a field scientist about to witness the antagonistic displays in the American *homo sapiens*?

Rosaline watched Hollister lace his arm through hers, smiling at the Lucas copy, "Sorry, she insisted we head to the dance floor."

"I didn't hear the lady ask you –" the FUBU snake growled low.

Supercop gave him an even smile. Rosaline tried to read that smile, not sure if she even should. Did Hollister get her silent cry for reinforcements?

"Don't worry, anything that's broken here I can fix that, *playa*." Hollister tossed over his shoulder as he led Rosaline to the dance floor like a gentleman.

The snake fumed in his rejection.

She gave him a parting smile. For once, it was nice to see Supercop.

*

"Are you okay, really?" Hollister asked her on the dance floor.

Rosaline nodded, moving to the Latin beats in step. "Yeah, he just got to me."

"Did he try to do something?" The cop voice came back.

Rosaline shook her head no.

Hollister nodded, moving slowly then warming up fully to the fast paced Brazilian dance music... Rosaline stopped a few times to see that Supercop could actually keep up with the hip-gyrating and heat in the music booming from the speakers.

The fast beats slowed to a romantic lull as Brazilian jazz poured from the speakers. Hollister gave her an air of uncertainty as some funny glances passed their way. She slipped her arms around his neck. He pulled back, but she gave him a nod of approval. He slipped his arms around her waist. They flowed together in the slow dance, moving a little too naturally together even for her...

“How long were you watching me?”

“Actually, I was getting a drink—after I watched him grab your arm.”

“Your timing was impeccable.”

“And if I didn’t come, do you think you would have been fine?”

“He was about to eat my heels, Supercop, but you scared him off.”

“Ok.”

“I don’t need a hero.”

“Never said you did.”

“And if you didn’t watch me all night?”

He hesitated then spoke. “Then, you would have handled yourself okay.”

“I just hated his arrogance. Like I was supposed to be so smoothed over by his game, I would fall into his bed that fast.” Rosaline felt her face warm at the memory. “Sorry, just thinking about how I met the first prick.”

“Don’t worry about wasting your energy. I won’t let another Lucas near you.”

A shiver ran down her arm. The one person she felt safe around stood in front of her on the dance floor. Rosaline nuzzled her head on his shoulder, closing her eyes... Instant electricity must have run through Hollister because he pulled back. “Rosaline, I don’t –”

“Shut up, Hollister, we’re dancing,” Rosaline ordered.

*

They threaded their way through the jungle of the good-byes after three in the morning. She led Hollister by the hand out of the party—which she dutifully dropped once they got to the end of the couple's driveway. He didn't make a sign that he knew or cared as he walked behind her all the way down the street until they reached his home.

"So you survived." Rosaline teased him as he reached for his house keys.

"I guess." Hollister looked like he survived a shoot-out.

"And you don't do parties? The way you moved on the dance floor, I think you've partied more than you want to admit."

"I don't normally do parties for good reason." Hollister opened the front door, his back to her while he said this.

"You're a man of too many good reasons." Rosaline folded her arms as they stepped inside. He hit a light in the living room as Rosaline sunk into the nearest seat. She snatched her heels off quickly, noting how badly her feet barked at her in pain.

Hollister took off his suede jacket, revealing the suave collared shirt beneath. *He dresses and acts normal enough in public but isn't social? How does that work?* She kept that question internal as she rubbed the balls of her feet with a free hand.

"The heels?" Hollister sat on the loveseat, leaning his head back.

"A good idea in my head, not a good idea for walking two blocks and dancing all night."

“They match the dress,” Hollister commented.

Rosaline smirked at how nervous he looked giving a compliment. “Fabulous!” she cried like Lovely when her friend would find a fashionable creation. The two laughed... Rosaline grew quiet... she saw her right arm near the red fabric of her dress... A memory of fire burnt into her conscience... the smell of her own burning flesh caught itself in her nose suddenly... her face must have turned because she stopped talking...

“What’s wrong?” Hollister must have sensed her mood change.

“I can’t cover everything.” Rosaline looked down, eyes getting moist.

The fire had only bought the worst out. It brought her to a place where she had to admit every pain, every strike.

“Your bruises?” They were back into territory each person mutually agreed to leave alone since the passing year closed. Rosaline dared to continue on this road. It would not go away. Denial only covered so much.

“Bruises, burns, how ugly I feel...”

“Stop. You were in a fire and just got out of an abusive relationship. Obviously, someone thought enough of you to hound you all the way to the dance floor. No one at the party paid attention to anything else but you.”

She fought the urge to lash out at Hollister for holding his pain together at least by glue and sticks more than she managed to, “I can’t keep pretending I’m having fun and that things don’t hurt me. Rosaline suddenly left the room, pulling her jewelry off. She stormed into the bathroom... Her right side still appeared freshly charred, faint reminders of Lucas and the harpies were on her left arm and back... she had just reached a place where she could look at herself absent clothing and not cringe. Make-up only went so far. Lying to herself only went so far. That dude at the party only wanted one thing. Everyone in her life only wanted one thing. Using her was okay to them... She covered her face while standing in front of the large mirror... Footsteps echoed from behind her...

Hollister must have come into the bathroom to talk to her. She glanced at him standing behind her. "I'm a monster," she whimpered, feeling his presence.

"You're not a monster. You're... scared and hurt. You're not ugly." His voice was so soft, so endearing. Her dad would speak like that. One of her foster dads spoke like that... they didn't take from her... A memory born of much shame and regret sparked in her mind.

The same twisted feeling washed over the adult Rosaline in the bathroom.

She wanted Hollister to touch her, to make her feel pretty.

"I'm sorry," she said as if Mr. Gary Blanchet stood in the room instead of Hollister.

"Are you okay?"

"The punch must have been special. I'm talking out of my head. I should go to bed."

Hollister remained concerned, judging by his voice, "If you want to talk –"

"Good night." Rosaline fled the room absent of her heels and her thoughts.

*

Rosaline made sure she didn't leave the guest room.

Because she would've knocked on his door, gone into his room, got into his bed... after five a.m., she called Lovely. Her mind was restless.

"Hello?" the sleepy voice answered after several rings.

"Lovely, I need to –" Rosaline began but was cut off by an angry voice.

"It's five in the morning," Lovely sounded like a mother bear robbed of her cubs.

"Isn't this your normal hour for a Saturday night?"

"Not when you're working your butt off to make a quota. I had spring fashions, prom dresses and had to do the books. I didn't close until after midnight."

"Sorry."

"What is this about?"

She sucked in a hesitant breath but began. "It's about him."

"Who? The bastard?"

"No, the guy I'm staying with."

So, you didn't sleep with your roommate?"

"No." The answer was plain and stern.

"Okay, problem solved. Let me sleep—"

“He’s a decent guy who has only been nice to me. Why am I the one that feels hot for him?”

“You’re lonely, I get it.”

“That’s not it.” Rosaline swept that idea under the conversational rug fast.

Lovely hit her from another angle, “Unless you’re falling for the dude.”

Rosaline didn’t answer.

“Blame your hormones and close quarters. Does *he* have a thing for *you*?”

“I don’t even know if he likes me as a person sometimes,” Rosaline groaned, shaking her head, “We can go at it and be really cutthroat.”

“Okay, then chalk it up to not getting any and hush.”

“But, he does things for me without even asking. It’s like he – he watches out for me. He makes sure I get home safe, he cooks. We went to a party tonight, danced and he didn’t try me once –”

“Dang, *I* should marry the dude.”

“Come on, be serious.”

“Don’t mistake kindness for something it’s not, like love. That’s my advice.”

“I never said I loved him –” Rosaline’s voice rose.

“Sounds like you want this to be something it’s not.”

“I just said I felt a moment of weakness.”

"I just don't want to see you get hurt again."

"Thanks for your concern." Rosaline felt her patience wearing as thin as the paper napkins soaked by punch then hung up. She lay awake until Sunday morning sunshine streamed through the window.

She clutched her pillow. Hollister never made demands given the heavy meaning of a marriage document.

Do you want love in a fake marriage, Rozy Raz?

Her father's face came to her.

Was she trying to duplicate his love in Hollister?

***

Chapter Eighteen: March 9, 2008.

Sunday afternoon, Hollister felt drained.

Even with the house quiet, he stared at the ceiling in his bedroom. The clock on his nightstand flashed two in the afternoon. Stupid party he thought as his sleeping schedule was in a frenzy. He had work tonight and his body protested soundly. Hitting the pillow, Hollister turned over in his bed, trying to block the subject that kept his mind busy all morning. Around five, he jolted awake and remembered he fell across the bed in the same clothes from the party. *The party.* Sounds of music and a vision of Rosaline dancing like a ray of light killed any chance he would get rest.

Hollister gave up and pulled himself into a normal person with a hot shower and coffee. He sucked down the rest of the contents in the mug and left the house.

*

Judging by the look on her face, Rosaline looked just as surprised as he did to see her in her place of business. She checked a clock in the store somewhere to get the time.

"Don't you work tonight? It's almost six."

"I flipped because of that party and now I'm paying for it."

Rosaline straightened the Easter decorated photo studio with its bright eggs and bunnies; the tiny space tucked away in the larger department store seemed to swallow her up here.

"You do realize I leave in twenty minutes, right?"

“I wasn’t sure how your day was going, so I stopped in to ask.”

“And you came in search of the latest photo package for the spring. Can I interest you?” She held up the stuffed bunny to him.

He pushed the bunny away. “I’ll decline.”

She smiled and placed the stuffed animal down lovingly. “Okay, since you’re now my ride instead of the bus, what’s next?”

“I guess dinner.”

“You cooked?”

“I’m sure the Cuban place by the house did.”

She placed a finger to his cheek, pouting. “You really are tired. Poor baby.”

He turned his head. It was getting harder to resist her touch. “You may need to drive.”

“I’ll bite. Let me finish closing the studio.”

*

The Cuban place had a cozy aura as Rosaline and Hollister slid into a booth before closing time and ordered. Rosaline took her vest off to reveal a blouse with a single silver butterfly on it. He managed to pull on some black slacks and a random shirt in the closet before leaving the house. Their server returned with black beans and pressed sandwiches as they sipped Cuban sodas.

As they plowed through the meal, Hollister kept sneaking glances at Rosaline.

He wanted to stay guarded, but guardedness did not seem right. *She's not yours to explain anything to,* his mind informed him.

"You didn't have to go to the party." Rosaline seemed to be answering one of his thoughts. His head snapped up from his plate. She placed her drink down. "I know you had a "thing" about it and I shouldn't have thrown a fit like a little kid."

"It's fine."

"I just – I don't know, wanted to get out. Be normal again..." Rosaline picked at the rest of her sandwich and took a small bite. "Guess we both have our reasons for why we don't live normal."

He sat his drink down, mentally chasing a rabbit her words produced. *His life*. The life he didn't want to live. "I just have my reasons. That's all."

They finished their meals, taking a last refill of their drinks.

Hollister took a short breath then looked up at her. "I've done a few different things in major crimes: sex crimes, domestic violence, etc. My last assignment with my friend, Leland, was as a street cop in narcotics until we both went to separate departments."

"Is he the one who calls all the time and hopes I pick up?" Rosaline smirked.

Hollister laughed. "Yeah, him. We were building a case against one of our own, Detective Reynolds." The name came out like a bitter herb in his mouth. "Leland calls him a "sheet," a good-old-boy racist who got on the force because he has family there. This same detective was taking bribes from dealers. Leland started the case, I made the phone calls. We thought we were being good cops, then... Reynolds got suspended and we felt like that was justice."

Rosaline swished the remainder of her drink around in the glass, "Go on."

"We caused a big shake-up and our mutual friend, Jeanne, got a promotion to fill in Reynolds' spot as lead detective. I went out to celebrate this victory one night with a friend who worked homicide, Andrew. Andrew is my current boss' brother. We went to a club. I didn't drink much back then, given my wonderful familial history, but had a Jack and Coke."

Hollister forgot the rest of his meal, not sure if Rosaline cared to listen or not, but happily to be talking. He pictured Ybor City that night in that smoky nightclub, the taste of liquor dancing on his tongue.

"Who is this from?" Hollister asked the bartender when he got the third drink.

The bartender pointed to a curvy Spanish woman, wearing blue lipstick, on the dance floor. She waved in a flirty manner. Raven-haired and sultry, her skin made him think of terracotta.

Detective Andrew Caffee slapped Hollister on the back. "Caliente!"

"I don't know, Drew. I've had too many drinks."

"You better drink it or she might go back to the land of make-believe."

Hollister downed the glass. By the time his sixth drink came, a sick feeling washed over him, "Drew, I don't feel so hot." He fanned himself with his shirt collar, his face and torso soaked damp from perspiration.

Drew looked his friend up and down, "You're raining under your clothes, man."

"I mean I don't feel good. I need to lie down"

"I think she's got you sweating." Drew pointed to the woman walking their way.

His generous admirer leaned against the bar, licking her lips at him. "Maybe we can have a private party, papi."

Hollister didn't know how to respond.

Drew had to bring him back to reality with a nudge, "I see a lonely club girl in need of my attention. See ya."

He looked up. Rosaline had her hand under her chin, staring at him.

"We all knew the bartender, so I asked for a place to cool off. The bartender told me to head upstairs. I started making my way up there then got dizzy. Figured I trashed myself so much, I couldn't drive home. My admirer and I talked for a minute before I sent her on."

"What's wrong, papi? Too hot?" His admirer had taken his arm to help steady him.

They stood outside of a door to a room upstairs. Before she could follow him inside, he stopped her. "I got it. Besides, my head's pounding." Hollister groaned.

"Did I send you too many drinks?" She cooed, fussing over him like a small child.

Hollister gave her a small smile, "No, I'm a big boy. I could've said no."

"I can help you." She reached for his shades but he stopped her.

"It's okay. I just need to be alone for a minute. Thank you."

She gave him a dejected look as he shut the door. The room got very, very dark.

Rosaline cut in. “So, what happened?”

“I blacked out.”

“And?” Rosaline urged him to continue, like he was telling a ghost story.

“I came to and she was standing over me.”

He saw the dim room again, heard the loud music of Ybor on a Friday night, felt the beat-up couch he laid on, recalling feeling disgusted by the fact that so many other drunks had passed out up here. Then he remembered the disgust he felt with himself after looking down to see his pants undone, figuring out that he had become a part of the filth.

“You’re not so shy.” Miss Blue Lipstick winked at him as she pulled down her skirt..

Hollister scrambled to his feet, but stumbled into a nearby table.

She folded her arms looking and pouted. “It’s okay, papi, relax.”

“What are you doing here?”

“Getting dressed, silly.” Her laughter spilled like her jewelry did over her bosom.

Hollister tried to stand, but fell back on the couch. His hands were too slippery to reach for a phone or a gun.

She leaned over him, touching his damp face. His glasses were gone.

He flinched, “I told you I wanted to be alone.” He slapped her hand away.

"You told me a lot of things. How you wanted it, how much you liked it." She purred each word in delight and popped her lips. "I came back to check up on you. You didn't say anything about being alone then. Don't even worry about leaving cash. You should be thanking your friend."

The way she giggled at him made him wonder if this was just a dream. Hollister grabbed a fist full of his hair, dazed. The whole night was a blur of liquor and confusion. Moments passed. The world was spinning out of control. "I'll kill Drew."

She sat on the couch next to him, deliberately crossing her legs. "No, no, your friend Jamie."

"What?"

"What do you think this was all about? Jamie said this was a peace offering after everything that happened." She pointed to herself in her silver metallic halter top and tight black skirt, then pointed to an object across the room—a web camera connected to a computer. "He said you would want to remember this."

Hollister felt his sour stomach sink below his knees. She sat back on the couch, emitting all her sexuality and all his damnation. Hollister threw up in the nearest trash can.

Leland rescued him once he escaped the room. His friend wasn't as gentle as his admirer, forcing him to take a drug test. And when the test popped positive for ecstasy, Leland threw him in an empty jail cell to make him sweat out the after effects.

"James Reynolds sent the pictures to my condo the week after. If I didn't remember anything about that night, he did. And he promised to jog my memory if I testified against him during the indictment."

His dinner date gasped loud enough to shake him.

The memory ceased. He was back in reality with Rosaline, who was still sitting across from him in the Cuban place. Hollister threw two twenties on the table and jumped up. “We should go.”

Hollister saw the staff waiting for them to take their leave. Rosaline followed him out as if in a daze. The two drove in complete silence until they reached his driveway. Rosaline stared into space as he fought to keep his mind on driving. He had a thousand should-haves, would-haves, and could-haves since that night. He should have stayed home, should have gone off with Leland, should have gotten the ride home...

Once inside, he changed quickly into his uniform in hopes to escape the house quickly.

Rosaline sat on the couch, clutching a pillow to her chest. “I’m sorry. You didn’t even know you were drugged.”

He looked away. “Stupid is not an excuse. I don’t want sympathy.”

Rosaline’s face balled up into an anger he didn’t expect to see. “You can’t be so disciplined that you don’t enjoy life—”

“You couldn’t control Lucas. Did *you* deserve that?”

She paused, looking as if she was reeling from that verbal shot. “And you went out with a friend and something bad happened. Your point?”

“That is my *point*. I went partying and almost cost myself a job. I’ve already done that—” He snatched his shades off. “I’m not perfect!”

Rosaline threw her hands up. “Just don’t act like you’ll never mess up again, Supercop! You’re not invincible!”

His tone was laden in a morbid darkness. “I’ve made other mistakes I can never take back.” His hands shook as he held the frames. “I need to go.” He threw the shades back on his face and reached for his keys.

She got off the couch and followed him. “So you’re going to run off like you did last time? You’re not going to deal with whatever demon you’re running from?”

“Oh, now, *you* want to talk about running?” He took Rosaline by the arms suddenly and shook her. “I should’ve kept *your* bruises out of *my* business. Maybe you could have held onto your lie a little longer.”

Rosaline peeled his hands away and pushed him back. Her voice dissolved into a whimper of defeat. “You don’t get it how much I…” Eyes shining, she fled to the safety of the guest room and slammed the door.

Hollister threw his keys at the wall and dropped into the nearest chair. That’s not what was supposed to go down. Regret hovered over him. Now he had mistakes and stupid words he couldn’t take back.

The thin walls amplified her crying.

*

Hollister slammed his car door. Work sucked, his body felt worn and he still hated himself for leaving the house when Rosaline was crying. *Punk.*

Being home didn't bring any sense of relief. The sun made its ascension into the sky.

Was she still home? Would she want to talk after this?

He reached for his cell phone and dialed the only person who seemed to make sense.

Mother Hutchins picked up after the third ring. "How are you, baby? It's early."

"I told my—friend about what happened between me and Baby Jane and—and still managed to make her cry on the same day." He filled her in on the details about Sunday.

Mother Hutchins kept silent on her end until he finished. "You're talking to the wrong person."

"I figured I could trust her. She knows things I never even told my ex."

"No, baby, I meant this Rosaline girl can't help you."

He ran a hand through his hair. He only gave Mother Hutchins key details about his friend. "Yeah, she's been through the ringer, but she came clean with me about her past life—"

"*Hollister,* two broken people can't make a whole thing."

"I'm already seeing the therapist, Mrs. Hutchins, because I want my job back—"

"How much do you tell the therapist? Do you talk about the Baby Jane girl, your people, being adopted?" Mother Hutchins's words started to weigh on him.

"No," he confessed.

"You gotta realize you're in pain first before you help someone else. She gotta do the same."

He hung up and leaned against his car for support.

Would misery stop being the other woman in his life?

***

Chapter Nineteen: March 10, 2008

Monday morning, Rosaline stood in the kitchen possessed by the need to make a homemade breakfast at seven in the morning. Hollister was a foodie. Food would be a good sentiment to heal their latest riff. Like the kind she saw in the cookbook opened in front of her, with fluffy biscuits and crispy-looking bacon that made her want to bite the picture.

Rosaline stared at the ingredients: Flour, milk, eggs, cooking spray, pork, a rolling pin.

As she turned the oven on to preheat, she remembered her ex bullying her one day in her apartment:

"You can't cook? Thought your sistah girls were born with mitts and grease. You got eggs and milk on your body. You should be able to make something."

"Didn't have a home to cook in, Lucas."

"Not my fault nobody wanted you." He laughed at her so hard, it cut her.

Rosaline pushed her sleeves back and got to work, determined to make the ingredients obey her commands.

*

Her cell phone began to sing to her from the guest room. Rosaline went to retrieve it, wondering why the timer had not gone off. She had the burner ready for the bacon. "Hello?"

“I have a pile of bills here for you the size of Raymond James Stadium. Some Mrs. Jones lady from your old apartment brought them. Not sure why you made her your emergency contact.”

“Lovely, wait. Don’t hang up.”

“Yes?”

“I didn’t mean to dump all my relationship junk on you then hang up. I’ve been so wrapped up in me; I haven’t even talked to you about Terrence or the shop or anything—”

“It’s cool.”

“You were right.” That was hard to say and Rosaline felt it. “I need to come clean with him. I go to bed each night holding a pillow. Not everyone has someone as good as Terrence.”

Lovely sighed at her boyfriend’s name. Terence Glen traveled with the stage plays he helped produce often. The two were a power couple in the making, with no trouble to touch them. “So forgive me for wanting more than rough sex with a drunk Lucas on a borrowed mattress.”

“Sex isn’t love,” Lovely spoke as if a confession.

“But, that’s what women do. We trade some sex for a little love.”

“Have you told this guy that you want something more? I hear it in your voice, Rozy Raz.”

“I haven’t... because I don’t know what I’m feeling...” Rosaline fought to suppress the strange scary ache following her since he left town at the beginning of the year. That feeling was turning into a deep screaming want that hungered to be fed.

Her nose picked up a burning smell. Rosaline ran out of the guest room.

"For the last time, what's wrong?" Lovely cried into the phone. "Answer me."

Rosaline dropped it, shock filtering throughout her body. Curls of white smoke poured from the kitchen. And smoke gave way to fire.

*

The cloud of smoke and her own screams shrouded her as she beat the fire back with a kitchen towel. She tried to turn the stove off, but red flames mocked her.

Something crashed. A door opened somewhere in the house. Two strong arms pulled her out of the house. She clutched the side of a pole holding up the carport. His car keys and duffel bag littered the concrete. A hissing sound barraged her ears along with the sound of things being thrown around. Several minutes later, Rosaline crawled to the opening where the back door was. It hung off the hinges at a crooked angle.

Supercop stood with his back to her, every muscle in his body coiled. The kitchen was still hazy. The oven looked like it had its mouth open in shock as the contents of her creation remained discarded on the floor, blackened. She burned the food while talking to Lovely!

Rosaline screamed like someone died instead of her burning the food.

Hollister ran outside to find her on her knees. He pulled her to her feet by her arms to search for her eyes. She shook so hard, he forced her to sit down on the front porch with him. Hollister's voice sheltered her in his concern. "Are you okay?"

"Ididn'tthinkIwasthatbadofacookbutweweretalkingsolongandIalmostburnedyourhousedown-"

"Slow down." He ordered.

She coughed a little then freaked. Fears of returning to hospital for respiratory trouble struck her.

"*Now* tell me what happened."

She finally met his eyes. "I made breakfast."

She felt his hard stare more than she saw it behind his shades. He exploded. "You nearly torched my house because you can't cook?" Hollister jumped to his feet, his arms flapped wildly as he gestured to the kitchen. "I had to break the door down to get to you!"

"I just wanted us to have something nice like a TV family." Rosaline stood up and smacked him in the shoulder. Shame coursed through her after realizing how pathetic and weak she felt at the situation—at being held by him. "Forget it. *Forget* I said anything or did anything—"

"Rosaline, *stop*." Hollister restrained her by the wrists and pulled her into a tight hug. "Please tell me you're okay. I'll take you to the ER if you need—"

"I'm fine." She grew tight with her anger and wiggled out his embrace. "Not that you care."

Something sounded clipped in his voice. "Don't say that."

"I'm not dead this time, so stop worrying about it." She stormed into the house to find the bathroom. Rosaline fought not to drink in his touch too deeply, gripping the sides of the sink.

His footsteps weren't far behind. "You've been thinking about your fire—"

She choked back her tears, determined not to waste them. "I don't own it. It's something that happened and I want to block it out. Just like I wanted to block out last night and this morning and anything else I've done to ruin your life."

He didn't answer. She escaped the bathroom before he could follow her.

*

When Rosaline came back to his place later that night, the kitchen door looked new as the fragrance of lemons engulfed the entire house. She dumped her purse on the table, studying how ordered and neat the kitchen looked. That was his life: when the messes came, he cleaned it until there wasn't a trace. Was the breakfast fire a hallucination?

She was used to sweeping her life's messes under a rug and pretending they weren't there.

Frustration clung to her like a perfume. Work wasn't any better as an escape. The silence of the house gave her no indication about how *he* felt.

On the counter top was a small white tin. Her curious nature led her to walk over and investigate. Inside the tin were two dozen homemade lemon cookies with a note: *A tasty apology.*

"Explains the smell." She told the empty kitchen then pushed herself on top of the counter to use it like a chair. "Sorry, Supercop, you'll have one more mess on your hands after I eat these." The first cookie melted on her tongue. "*Mmmm.* I'm a girl with a lot of pain to feed." She reached for a second one, allowing her thoughts to melt in her mind… The sound of a door opening and closing perked her ears. Half of the cookies were gone. Crumbs dusted her fingers. *Too late to pretend I'm not here*, she thought, then continued on the next dozen.

Hollister came into the kitchen, halted in his steps then cleared his throat. "Evening," he began while throwing his work jacket on the back of a chair.

"Hi," She gave a cherry reply to suppress asking why he had not changed out of his uniform.

He folded his arms. “How’s my counter?”

“Shiny. You’re very neat.” She spoke with a piece of cookie in her mouth, suddenly remembering to wipe the crumbs away with a free hand from the corner of her mouth.

He closed the gap between them. “Do you need help getting down? My chairs seem to work fine as places to sit in and I spent a good portion of my day cleaning.”

“Nope.” She ate the last bite and smiled, fancying herself a kitten with her paw in a fish bowl.

Hollister sighed. “It’s hard to ruin something that’s already messed up.”

“Really, Hollister, I’ll clean the kitchen up—”

“I don’t mean the kitchen.” A rough hand rested on her cheek. “I was wrong for throwing my life out to you, then expecting you to sort it out. It was a serious foul and I’m sorry.”

Rosaline gently pushed his hand away and looked down. “I should go to bed—”

“Why haven’t you left yet?”

Her head snapped up. Such a question dumped another layer of confusion on their entanglement.

“You have enough talent as a photographer to work somewhere else other than a department store. Cash isn’t the issue. The marriage license is just a dead tree in my lockbox.” She could see his dark eyes over the rims of his sunglasses. “I don’t need to help you or protect you anymore.”

She opened her mouth but couldn’t speak. *I’m stranded on your island with nowhere to go.*

Her feelings for Mr. Liano were going to be like the lemon cookies: savored until gone.

***

Chapter Twenty: March 10, 2008

Hollister's fuzzy brain told him to leave such heavy questions alone. He had spent his day fighting for snatches of sleep and cleaning the kitchen after the minor fire. The repair bill for the back door meant nothing. Two nights off awaited him. The need to rest was demanding his attention—so was the answer to his question.

Rosaline reached out and pulled at the blue tie of his uniform. The knot unraveled from her tug. Now a funny knot formed in his throat. He was more than just a little confused. The weight of his own humanity dropped on him.

"What are you doing?" He pulled back some.

"Doing what?" she asked as if nothing happened.

"Was my tie bothering you?" A slight annoyance tinted his tone.

"Other than the fact it's ugly as sin," she laughed.

He shook his head. "I'm not awake enough to play."

"You need to loosen your tie more." She crossed her legs and smirked.

"Rosaline." Somewhere in that exchange, they stopped talking about his uniform.

She reached for his shades.

His hands automatically blocked hers.

Rosaline frowned. "You really don't get that you have nice eyes." She reached for the sunglasses.

He restrained her by the wrists. His grip was firm enough to warn her that her comedy was way past his comfort zone. "Stop."

He released his grip—only to have her move a fraction faster than he did and used her free hand to get the shades. Now he was looking at Rosaline without them, blinking hard in the soft light of the kitchen.

He loathed the feeling of being without protection as he reached for them.

She kept them out of reach. "Stop hiding behind these stupid things."

"I need those to see."

"For medical purposes, but not to hide."

"Rosaline, game over."

"You have a gun. You can get them back. *Trust me.*"

"I'm not in the mood for this. I just wanted to apologize and have a serious conversation so we knew where we stood after this."

She held his gaze. "What are you so afraid of? It's not the thought of me leaving."

He slammed both palms on the countertop, trapping her between him and the wood grain. "Save the mental games for a shrink."

She placed the sunglasses behind her back. “These glasses are a cover.”

“Just like that hair dye you wear that’s the color of a fire engine. Black kettle, black pot.”

Rosaline shrugged and slid off the counter.

He loomed over her.

“What are we so afraid of to see within each other? Scars? Shame? Pain?” She sighed. “We can call each other out, but we still keep covering up what’s so obvious in us.”

“Thanks for the moment of clarity, but hand me the shades back,” he growled.

Her eyes narrowed. “When are you going to be something else than Supercop?”

He broke his gaze. Now she hit him in a wounded spot. This woman didn’t fight fair. The sunglasses were another thing in his life designed to help him keep his control, his structure. His structured life kept the demons at bay.

“The last time I let go—” He started. *The last time I let go, I was with a woman.*

“The last time *I* let go, I got a black eye. The last time I let go, I didn’t know how much of a waste Lucas was. The last time you let go, you made a mistake. Things happen! You erred on the side of caution so much that you stopped living.”

His mouth dried up as his heat pounded in his chest. All the mistakes he made when he let go rushed to his memory—enjoying kisses from Baby Jane’s blue-painted lips, taking in a half-dead redhead, killing a man, being the sissy Han called him…

Hollister wanted to be released of such heaviness like a butterfly being freed from someone's hand. "I don't want people to see how pathetic I really am."

Rosaline tilted his face up toward hers with both hands. "So you just stop letting anybody in."

"When I let my guard down –" He choked up some.

"Then you'll be human like the rest of us," Rosaline finished. "Guess what? *You're* in my life and I'm messed up, too." A sad light filled her eyes as she slipped the glasses back on his face.

An inward groan escaped him. His eyes wrote out feelings too heavy to share, but too strong to keep internal. "I can't keep thinking that we have a chance."

He wondered if she grabbed his tie for leverage because she looked faint. "Hollister, I—" she uttered a word but couldn't finish.

He drank up her mahogany eyes brimming with something her lips couldn't say. This part wasn't a game. His world spun on the very implication of her being here. "Rosaline, I need you."

She pulled him by his tie closer to her face, her lower back against the counter.

Rosaline pressed her lips to his in a moment he failed to comprehend, but he let go enough to respond to it. Hollister picked Rosaline up in his arms, cradling her as carefully as he hoped to be with her emotions. He carried her out of the kitchen the way he should have if they had a real wedding, carrying her over an invisible threshold that separated them for this long.

Hollister wrapped her in an embrace tailored with the desperation of his affections, kissing her deep enough to drink up whatever passions possessed her.

*

When he woke again, Hollister heard the rain falling on the roof.

Seasons were changing to prepare the flowers longing to bloom. Rosaline gave him that impression: a flower waiting to bloom, a butterfly ready to become more than something trapped in a cocoon…a cell phone ringing took him out of his beautiful musings.

He opened his eyes in the room only illuminated by the flashes of lighting outside.

Was it morning already?

Rosaline was leaning down, digging her cell phone out of a pocket in her jeans that were discarded on the tiled floor. Her red hair flirted with the nape of her neck, bringing back a rush of memories—how the scent of her lavender body wash tangled with his sandalwood cologne, the softness of her hair, the sweetness of her skin despite the trail of old bruises and burns.

"Hello? Yes, this is she…it's what time? Oh my…I'm *so* sorry, I didn't…I'll be there asap to open the studio…I know, I know…look, let me get dressed….I didn't mean to oversleep…" She disconnected. "Crap. She hung up."

He reached over and touched her shoulder. "What's wrong?"

She turned to look at him, hand on her forehead. "It's nine in the morning. I was supposed to be at the studio early." She cursed. "And I missed my bus—"

"I'll take you to work." He quickly added.

She slipped out from under the blanket and got off the couch, heading toward the bathroom. It took him another fifteen minutes to come to earth, still in a daze after last night. He tossed on a pair of worn jeans and a shirt as she rushed through her normal beauty ritual.

Ten minutes after that, they were going down the highway as fast as possible with the bad weather being a major factor. As soon as his car pulled up into the department store parking lot, Rosaline jumped out and ran through the rain, her umbrella clutched tight to her hand.

*

Hollister stood under the icy water in the shower so long, he wondered if he could become a jungle Popsicle... the turn of events ran down his mind like the water ran down his naked back. He finally stepped out and grabbed a towel.

Why did she let *him*?

He shook himself, staring absent-mindedly at his damp ebony locks in the foggy mirror. Hollister sighed loud enough to fill the empty house.

Why think when it was better to *feel*?

Rosaline eliminated the last time factor. The last time he let go translated into the last time they could pass through his house simply married in name.

She had dozed off in his arms last night as he held her. His heart overjoyed that he was given the chance to share all of the comfort and caring built up inside when they became tangled up in each other.

He leaned against the bathroom wall and got lost in his thoughts about last night.

Just like with her safety, Hollister wanted to make sure he was careful with Rosaline.

***

Chapter Twenty-One: March 11, 2008

Checker players shouldn't play chess.

Somewhere this great tidbit of wisdom from her father followed Rosaline through the years. She walked around the mall after her shift ended, comparing her relationship with Hollister to a chess game: She moved. He moved. Then she wanted to stop playing his wife after she realized she kissed him. His kiss stepped up the intensity, leading to them sealing the sincerity of their matrimony in the most intimate way… The store assistant manager chewed her out for being late. She apologized over and over and then threw herself into work, promising to take pictures for the upcoming commercial holidays—Mother's Day, Father's Day, graduations, proms.

The way the time had passed at work wasn't like how time passed with Hollister—being kissed, being held. Loved on, loved into. *Happy.* She spent last night being happy. Rationality collided with her dreaming—she wanted to tell him she was lonely and that's why she did it. So she could feel desired somehow. She didn't want him to fall for her.

A part of her reasoned that they were two adults dealing with hormones and that's how it worked out... she was safe, she imagined, in his mind, just someone to be safe with. No judgmental girlfriends or eccentric whores. He struggled with demons in romance and childhood similar to hers... Rosaline wanted to label this as a physical thing... he wanted to be valued as a human, too.

He wanted to be Detective Liano, not an abused foreigner with a dead mother.

Just like her. He was her.

She wanted to be more than Lela's cast-off and the failure of the foster system. Rosaline never felt good enough or pretty enough or worthy enough for a good thing... Then Hollister told her he needed her, making her feel wanted. She couldn't shake something she yearned for this long in life.

Rosaline reached the end of the mall, realizing she only had ten minutes to get to her bus stop.

She, a lowly checker player, needed to make a move.

*

Rosaline let herself into Hollister's house, telling herself she was strong enough to work through this pseudo-relationship stuff. They were two adults who were going to talk like adults and find that closure stuff both of them needed. The empowerment speech was written in her head well before Hollister came into the living room in only his pajamas and a tank top — and his broad shoulders successfully erased the whole speech. The slightly spiked hair, the fabled sunglasses, the touches of cologne scented like sandalwood. Police academy must have treated him well as the cotton in the tank top clung to chiseled pecs and rock-solid abs, arms boasting well-defined biceps eager to hold her. No wonder she fell asleep in anatomy class in high school because right now she clearly appreciated the perfect male figure right in front of her… Rosaline forced herself to straighten up. *Stop thinking about him, stupid…*

He looked more relaxed now. "I wasn't sure if I should have called you. I know your shift ended a couple hours ago. You know, with the rain and all—"

"I just needed a minute to myself." Rosaline tried to be aloof, heading for the guest room. She changed into a pair of shorts and a baby tee before marching back into the living room.

A funny tension came back into the air. He sat on the couch as if waiting for her.

She stopped. Stupid couch and stupid sexy memories attached to it.

“We should talk.” His voice held an authority he was used to having.

“Okay.” Rosaline readied herself and stayed on her feet.

“Last night–”

“Yeah?” Rosaline waited. Would he say what she thought? The rational part? Cutting her down would have been a hard yet acceptable alternative.

“I don’t regret last night.” He moved on the verbal chessboard.

“I’ll only regret it if I’ve placed you in an awkward position. The marriage thing is weird all on its own. Your staying doesn’t require more than seeing your life get better. If you decided to leave, I understand.”

“I’ll remember that.” Now she had to make another move. “Hollister –” Rosaline began but he held up a hand.

“You’re worth the trouble to me.”

“I made a move that I regret, Hollister, I moved too fast—”

“You’re not a whore to me,” Hollister quickly added, standing up on his bare feet. “I want to show you that *I* respect you.”

Rosaline folded her arms. “Do you respect me enough *not* to only expect something physical?”

“Yes. You deserve to be happy and do what is right for you. Even if I’m not a part of that.”

She felt her demeanor crack, a thoughtful pause followed. Rosaline shook herself, “You could have said no. Or did the lack of *no* have anything to do with the fact that you’re still a man living with a woman?”

Hollister looked down, shaking his head. He bit his lip and ran a hand through his hair, then met her stare. “Not every man gets the chance to make love to you. I thought I got that.”

His move cemented his victory in this strange game they played.

Sex wasn’t love. Lovely’s conversation burned into her brain.

Rosaline was so familiar with people taking from her that she failed to see anyone offering anything back. Skewed notions of intimacy led to many wrong turns, especially with Lucas.

Yet, Hollister wanted to *make love to her*?

Rosaline walked up to Hollister. She took his shades off his face, this time without much resistance on his part. His inky colored eyes wrote out deep questions that she didn’t have verbal answers to. She pulled him toward the back of the house by one hand and kept his sunglasses in the other.

*

Evening became night. The sound of the rain returning to wash the world in a late downpour woke Rosaline up. The clock on the nightstand indicated that it was after midnight. She looked up at Hollister with one of his arms locked behind his head and his face pointed toward the ceiling.

Shifting in the bed, she turned toward him. “What’s wrong?”

Even in the dim room, it was weird seeing him without the sunglasses. Every expression that came across his face seemed amplified. “I don’t want to be the monster my father was.”

She leaned on her elbow. “Monsters don’t talk like you, Supercop.”

He licked his lips then shook his head. “What he did to my own mother, his own wife—”

“I know you’ll be careful with me.”

“I still have my secrets—” his voice dropped.

“No deep, dark secrets permitted right now, please. We’ve shocked each other enough.”

He turned his face toward hers. “You deserve to be happy.”

“Hollister, you’re not your dad and you’re not Lucas.”

“Please don’t let me be. I don’t know how to be a man. At least not one strong enough to give you what you need. I’m afraid of being less than what you make of me.”

Rosaline stared into his eyes. “Stop thinking you’ll mess up. You’re *not* too messed up for me.”

“When you have a good thing—” Hollister kissed her on the forehead. “Right now, you mean everything.”

Everything was new territory to a girl who always meant nothing to so many others. Rosaline leaned over and pressed her lips against his, ready to give him everything she had left.

***

www.ingramcontent.com/pod-product-compliance
Lightning Source LLC
LaVergne TN
LVHW080552160826
845677LV00010B/1819
* 9 7 9 8 7 7 3 1 7 2 3 0 7 *